An Unexpected Affair

Affair

SCOTTISH WEREBEARS BOOK 1

LORELEI MOONE

CONTENTS

CHAPTER ONE

Throughout her flight into Inverness, Scotland, Clarice found herself repeatedly going over the printout she'd taken of her destination: Moss Cottage on the Isle of Skye. It promised unspoiled vistas, a homely atmosphere and most importantly of all: a quiet getaway from the hustle and bustle of modern life.

That's what she needed most: to get away. Away from the distractions of life in London, away from the constant buzz of her phone, notifying her of incoming emails or tweets. Away from all reminders of the life she used to share with Alan before she caught him cheating on her.

Upon her arrival at the cottage, she would send a message to Lily, her best friend, who had also been the one to suggest the Isle of Skye as a destination to begin with, and that was it. Clarice had promised herself to switch everything off. From nine to five daily, she would be *unplugged*, allowing her to focus on the task at hand.

After stealing a glance out the window - they were still descending through thick cloud cover - she flipped the page over, reading the backside again. *Local attractions include wildlife walks, beach walks, hill trails.* Walks, basically, all you could do on the Isle of Skye according to this text was go for a quiet walk.

It is going to have electricity, though, won't it? Clarice read the other side again and studied the accompanying pictures. There was a table lamp in one of the shots, which suggested that electricity was indeed going to be supplied... As long as her laptop had power, everything was going to be all right.

As the small plane landed bumpily on the runway, she felt a surge of excitement as well as nerves build within her chest. Soon, a mere three-hour drive away, she was going to arrive at her destination.

"Please remain seated until the fasten seatbelt sign is switched off," said the captain's almost robotic voice over the intercom.

Clarice smiled to herself. N*o way that's going to happen.* Half these people would be up, carry-on luggage and phone in hand, before the plane came to a halt.

She leaned over to get a better look out the window. The views throughout most of the flight had been obstructed by a thick layer of clouds, far below the altitude of the plane. Now, the outside world looked as one would expect Scotland to look in early autumn: grey and damp.

How does it matter, it's not like I'll leave the house, much. Clarice took a deep breath, holding it in an attempt to calm her nerves. She had never done anything like this. Leave it all behind for a few weeks of solitude.

But this time, it was necessary. Early attempts to figure out if there was any flexibility in the deadline for her latest book had only resulted in her editor breathing down her neck harder. Apparently anything short of a deadly illness wasn't cause enough to postpone a release. A messy breakup and resulting existential crisis didn't count. That was why Clarice had been forced to resort to drastic measures to finish the manuscript on time.

Finally, the fasten seatbelt signs switched off with the customary ding, and soon after, the doors of the plane opened. Clarice smiled a final goodbye to the quiet old man seated next to her. The flight was relatively short, as far as flights go, but she was still surprised that he hadn't said a word throughout. He nodded, then joined the throng of impatient passengers heading for the door.

It was a small airport, meaning you didn't get one of those fancy walkways leading from the plane straight to the door. Instead, all the passengers were let off via a mobile staircase, and then they walked along demarcated pathways painted on the concrete taxiway, towards the modest looking terminal building to collect their bags.

The bags arrived in a similarly low-tech manner: on trolleys in plain view of the waiting passengers. Clarice found her suitcase and started walking, aimlessly at first, until she spied the car rental sign.

Alan used to take care of all of these things during their holidays together, but now it was all up to her. *How hard can it be?*

As it turned out, picking up a pre-booked rental car wasn't very difficult at all. However, Clarice was still battling residual nerves by the time she made it into the driver's seat and started leafing through the various printouts of the route to the Isle of Skye. It looked easy enough, there weren't very many roads to choose from. The maps on Clarice's phone concurred.

A deep breath later, she turned the key. So far so good, now it was time for the home stretch.

———◦◆◦———

As pretty as the drive towards the Isle of Skye was, it did nothing to prepare her for the beauty ahead. Stark black cliffs stood out against the dramatic clouds overhead. There wasn't much vegetation, just grasses and mosses with the occasional small grouping of trees that had managed to battle the elements for survival.

Though the road snaked through the landscape up ahead, Clarice still felt like an explorer, discovering this mysterious land for the first time. At every bend, she instinctively slowed, both to cater for oncoming vehicles - which were few and far between - as well as to admire the views.

She passed through a few small towns on the way, but for the most part, the island seemed unspoiled and almost barren. The road narrowed more and more as she reluctantly drove on. Every map she'd printed out, even the satellite navigation on her phone confirmed she was on the right track, yet the road ahead looked too small to lead anywhere.

Finally, she made it to a small settlement that according to Google was a mere twenty minutes away from her destination. *Village* would be too big a word for the cluster of houses she found. Luckily one of the buildings housed a small daily needs shop. Clarice parked right outside, eager to stock up on some essentials so she wouldn't have to leave the cottage at least for the next couple of days.

"Hello?" she called out through the open door.

No answer.

She stuck her head inside, looking around the dimly lit interior of the store. It looked like somebody's living room, with a few racks of groceries, as well as firewood and some camping supplies stacked up inside.

"Excuse me?" she asked again.

Finally, an old man appeared through the door at the far end of the room.

"Ah, a customer!" He shot her a smile that seemed to wrinkle up every inch of his face all at once. "How can I help?"

"I just wanted to buy a few things," Clarice explained, smiling nervously while eyeing the shelf of cookies nearer the wall.

"Aye, of course. Please take a look around. If you're

after anything specific, we may need to order it in."

Clarice nodded and gathered up some packets of digestives. It was a bad habit, snacking while writing, especially when writing was your main job and you spend a lot of time doing it. With the deadline hanging over her head, she didn't know how else to cope.

She rounded off her selection with some bread, eggs, and other daily essentials, then made her way towards the counter where the old man was waiting. He didn't even have a till. Instead he listed up everything on a notepad and totaled it in his head.

"Where are you staying, if I may ask?" He handed her the torn off sheet of paper, with the total, £20.78 written in shaky pencil.

Clarice paused for a moment, wondering if it was wise to answer. *What the hell, this place is so small, he would probably find out anyway. You're not in London anymore!*

"Moss Cottage. That's just up the road I suppose?"

"Ah yes. The old McMillan farm. Lovely place, very quiet. Just-" He leaned forward, raising his hand gravely. "Take care of the bear."

"Thanks. Umm, wait, what bear?" Clarice asked.

"Up in the hills around the farm. Keep your eyes open if you go wandering out by yourself. Especially in the evenings."

Clarice scrutinized the old man's face, looking for any sign that he was just pulling her leg, but his expression remained completely serious.

"I wasn't aware that there were bears in Scotland?"

The old man let out a chuckle. "Well, according to the authorities, there aren't any, but we've all seen him. A big fella too, could tear you in half, he could." By the end of his sentence, again the old man's expression turned deadly serious.

"But enough of that, you seem like a sensible lass, you'll be careful. Enjoy your vacation." He smiled again, his weathered skin folding into a million little creases.

"Uhh, thanks."

"Bye now!"

Back at the car, Clarice tried to shake off her unease at the preceding conversation. *A bear. Here? That's ridiculous, right?* As far as she knew, bears had been extinct in Britain for pretty much forever. Unless it was some kind of zoo escapee.

No, perhaps the old man had been enjoying his Scotch a bit too much. That must be it.

CHAPTER TWO

McMillan Farm had been in Derek's family for generations. He was born there, grew up there, and was likely going to die there if he had his way. Ever since his parents' passing many years ago, the farm had been mostly Derek's responsibility. Sure, he had an older brother, but Aidan preferred to travel the world rather than stay home and tend the land, and as such only came by a few times a year.

Derek's farm was the perfect place for a bear, actually, that's why his ancestors moved here two centuries ago, and why he was never tempted to leave like his brother. The vast countryside gave him plenty of space to roam. The rivulet carving its way through his property provided ample opportunity to fish when the season was right, and the best part was, there weren't many people around.

The only people that did turn up were paying guests: mostly middle-aged or older couples, or the occasional young family that was trying to teach their children about nature. Avoiding them when the urge to shift took over was quite easy. He'd never been caught, which was fortunate, because all bears lived by the code of secrecy.

The holiday cottages were set away from the main farmhouse by a safe distance, and visitors were mostly self-sufficient. All Derek did was make sure everything was in working condition and provide some basic supplies. Although it wasn't ideal, inviting strangers into his territory, it was his way of earning a little extra money from his land without much effort.

This month's visitor was probably going to be the

same. Clarice Adler from London.

The name had conjured up images of white permed hair and floral dresses in Derek's mind. A posh old lady, no doubt, who he imagined used to spend her younger days riding horses in the English countryside before moving to London. Her insistence in the comment box of the booking form that her stay should be as quiet and undisturbed as possible only supported his assumptions. This was going to be someone who had grown up in the country, who was now yearning to get back to a simpler life for two weeks.

When her grey rented hatchback slowly crawled through his main gate, he didn't need to sneak a peek to know what she'd look like. After fifteen years in the tourism business, his instincts were always right, so he kept on mowing the lawn as if he hadn't noticed the new arrival.

The car came to a halt a little way up the drive, and then it turned left, following the signs he had put up last winter, leading to the cottages. Derek had already prepared Moss Cottage for its latest guest. The bed was made, the pantry was stocked, and the key was in the front door.

Although he did often check in with visitors on the first day, just to see to it that they were comfortable, he preferred to play as small a role as possible in their visit. It wasn't that Derek disliked the tourists, he was just a very private person.

When he was done with the lawn in front of the house, he prepared himself for his regular evening routine: check on the bees as well as the other animals, take a round of the kitchen garden to harvest the last of the summer crops to add to his winter stash, perhaps say hello to the visitor before retreating to the farm house to prepare a nice cut of meat for dinner.

"Hello? Is anybody here?" a clear female voice called

out to Derek from outside the barn where he had just parked the lawn mower.

He wiped his hands clean on his overalls, then marched out to greet what he assumed must have been the old lady staying at Moss Cottage. Nothing could prepare him for what he saw waiting for him outside, though.

The shapely woman with brunette hair standing in front of him couldn't have been older than thirty at the most. Her amber eyes flitted back and forth skittishly between him and the surrounding trees as she waited for him to reach her.

It took a lot of focus for him to remember the usual niceties city folk expected.

"Derek McMillan. Nice to meet you," Derek said, sticking out his hand to greet his guest.

Though he tried not to stare, her feminine curves invited a closer look. Instead of acting rude, he tried to focus on her face. High cheek bones, full lips, almond-shaped, kind eyes. Perfection.

"Oh. Clarice. Just call me Clarice." She hesitated for a moment with her arms hanging down her sides but finally took his much larger hand anyway.

It was as if an electric current passed between the two when their fingers first touched, but she barely reacted - at least not favorably. In fact, she pulled her almost fragile little hand back almost possessively after the shortest of greetings. That proved it; the attraction was definitely not mutual.

"Is there anything I can help you with? Did you find the cottage to your liking?" Derek asked.

Her eyes met his for a split second, but then she looked away again. Her demeanor reminded him of prey, painfully aware of the danger it was in. And her scent was more enticing, lovelier than a summer meadow in full bloom.

There was something about her that he couldn't put his finger on. Something tempting that made the most primal part of his being want to own her.

"I..." she began, but then fell silent again.

In all his years running the cottages, he'd never found himself in an awkward position like this. Sure, he'd had as many female guests as male ones over the years, but never one who affected him so. Humans didn't hold much interest for him - not until right this moment - neither did most of his own kind for that matter. He had always been happily solitary: a bachelor by choice as well as circumstance.

Bears didn't live in large packs like wolves did, and they favored vast territories all to themselves. That was one of the reasons his kind was dwindling; they simply didn't get the opportunity to pair up often enough.

"Yes?" he asked.

His reaction to her was visceral, involuntary, and completely undesirable. The longer he stood in front of her, the more difficult was it for him to suppress his instincts and remain civil. All he wanted to do was pounce. Take her into his arms and make her his.

He didn't understand it, how a human could have this effect on him. Everything he felt, how the bear in him threatened to take over with every breath he took, made the hair on his forearms stand up. It felt like something he'd heard about a long time ago. But that kind of behavior was limited to bears and their mates. It didn't apply to human women, did it? Perhaps he had kept himself isolated for too long, and his instincts were rusty...

For once he wished Aidan was around. Since his brother was much more well-traveled, he might have had advice for Derek, but it was up to him alone to sort out this mess.

The next couple of weeks were going to be difficult, if not impossible.

"I just wanted to say hello. And to thank your wife... for the cake you left on the dining table. A lovely gesture."

He was about to interject that he wasn't married, but restrained himself, his hand instinctively reaching for a non-existent itch on his chin instead. So what if she mistakenly assumed another female presence had baked that cake to welcome her? Even though it pained him to let her think that there was someone else in his life, at least it would provide him with excuses to keep even more of a distance than he usually did with visitors.

"You're welcome. Now I'd best get back to work."

"Of course. Don't let me keep you. Thanks again."

He nodded at her and almost fled back into the barn. In fifteen years, he'd never been wrong at sizing up his guests from names and booking information alone. Had he had any indication that she would affect him like this, he would have canceled the reservation in a heartbeat.

In one afternoon, everything he had previously known to be true about himself had changed. No longer was he the stoic, practical bear he thought he was. She had awoken something in him that he never knew existed. A dangerous urge he'd heard spoken of in stories his parents used to tell when he was only a cub.

He regretted not being able to ask them for an explanation either, for advice on how to handle the situation. But they died a long time ago, and Aidan was God knows where.

Either way, Clarice Adler was here to stay, at least for the next couple of weeks. Derek couldn't yet guess just how much of an effect Clarice's presence at McMillan Farm would have on his life going forward.

CHAPTER THREE

Clarice was still reeling with the after effects of her meeting with Derek as she wandered back up the gravel path towards her cottage. The short exchange with the bearded stranger had left her completely off kilter. He was a handsome man, in a raw, extremely masculine sort of way. Broad, no doubt strong after years of physical work on the farm. Big hands, bigger arms. His wife must be one lucky woman.

She chided herself for objectifying the man. If someone ever admitted to thinking about her that way, she'd be offended - not that anyone did think of her that way. And yet, her thoughts couldn't help but return to the gutter even as she locked herself inside the cottage, closing the curtains in an attempt to isolate herself. Yet that dirty part of her brain, which insisted on feeding her speculations of how Derek McMillan might be in the sack, refused to switch off completely.

It had been a while, sure. Even before kicking Alan to the curb just after Valentine's Day, they hadn't shared a bed for at least a month as things had cooled off between them. While she was quite sure that things were pretty much over before he stepped out on her, part of her had kept wondering if it was all her fault. Perhaps she should have tried harder to keep the magic alive?

Stop it, that's the kind of thinking that makes a girl desperate.

Desperation was indeed pretty close to how Clarice felt now. Giddy like a school girl coming face-to-face with an unrequited crush. Her heart was still racing when she remembered the one thing she had gone to ask Derek about: cell phone reception. *Damn.*

The slightly stand-offish manner in which he'd interacted with her, plus her confused desires discouraged Clarice from going back and talking to Derek again. Plus, knowing her luck, she would probably find herself tongue-tied and swooning over the man, with a jealous wife looking on from inside the farmhouse. That sort of thing was bound to make her two-week stay even more awkward. *No thanks.*

Clarice decided to make herself a cup of tea and enjoy a slice of the still warm, slightly sticky lemon and honey cake along with it. Once revitalized, and slightly more in control of herself and her impulses, she decided to go out for a walk. Perhaps if she backtracked the way to the village on foot, she could find a spot where her phone worked long enough to make a quick call to Lily.

The lack of network around the cottage wasn't such a bad thing. A blessing in disguise, Clarice thought, as she turned onto the main road outside the gate. There was no way she would be tempted to check her phone during working hours if she didn't have any signal in the first place.

Still, until she could get in touch with Lily to let her know she'd arrived safely, it was a bit of a nuisance. The village wasn't far, at least it hadn't seemed far in the car. But now that she was walking on the narrow road, through the little wooded patch outside the farm boundary, she felt as though she was completely cut off.

Unlike where she lived in London, here, a car was an absolute must, she could see that now. But she was determined to soldier on a bit further down the road to see if she couldn't find a connection at least for a short while. Even if it was just one bar on her phone, that would be enough to send a quick text message, right?

In her eagerness to get word out, she started typing it already while walking, not paying much attention to the road surface underfoot, or the views around her.

Dear Lily, I'm here but have crap network so am doing this real quick by text. Don't worry about me. The place is lovely, and I'll get loads done here. Love, C.

Send.

Clarice kept staring at the screen as the phone attempted to send the message without any signal. She continued along the winding road for another five minutes, almost stumbling into a pothole on the way. Then the tree cover opened up. The view stretched out ahead of her, revealing grasslands and even a bit of dramatic coastline in the distance.

Her phone also seemed able to 'see' much better from here, despite the thick gray clouds overhead, and the message finally went through.

What a relief.

Clarice put the phone in her handbag and looked around properly now. It really was a beautiful place, this island. The fact that there was not a soul around was eerie and enchanting in equal measures. As she kept standing there in the same spot for another few minutes, a chill seemed to pass over the landscape, signaling the arrival of dusk. It wasn't very late yet, but the clouds made it seem much darker than it should have been, and the wind had picked up slightly as well.

Time to head back.

Clarice turned, when from the corner of her eye she thought she could see movement in the trees. She didn't manage to see it properly, but it looked big. Much bigger than a person. Startled, she clutched her handbag tightly to her chest and just tried to remain calm. *Deep breaths. It's probably nothing.*

But her instincts, however frazzled, insisted that it *was* something. She could practically hear the old man from the village store warn her about that bear all over again. What if he was right? What if on her first evening here, she came face to face with a fierce beast that would eat her alive? With her car parked outside the cottage, Derek or his wife would just assume she was still inside. There was no telling when - *if* - her body would be found!

She stood deadly still for another minute or so, scanning the trees around the road she'd just come from. Although they were only medium sized trees, and not very densely planted, the gaps between them were quite dark already. As if night had fallen early. All around her seemed quiet, though. Her frantic heartbeat slowed slightly.

Perhaps she had just imagined it. She took another deep breath and tried to banish all remaining thoughts of bears and danger from her mind. She had to get back before it got really dark.

Step by step, reluctantly at first, she walked back into the woods, careful to avoid fallen twigs and other debris on the road that would make noise if she stepped on them. As she grew more confident that she was alone, she sped up, eager to return to the safety of the farm. She had just imagined it. There was nothing in these woods! She was just being ridiculous. The over-active imagination that made her a good writer could be a curse at times like these.

The road wound left to right and back again, never revealing more of what lay ahead of the next turn. She didn't recognize it really, but then how could she? Things looked different in this light, and she hadn't paid much attention while walking earlier, because she was trying to type out that message to Lily.

She continued on for five, six minutes, growing more and more worried that perhaps she'd gotten lost somehow. Finally, she spied a sign up ahead. McMillan Farm. *Thank God.*

As she passed through the gates that lay just beyond the next bend, she turned back one last time. Through the dark passage among the trees, a distant roar sent shivers down her spine. It made way for more silence so soon after that she doubted she'd actually heard it. Her mind was playing tricks on her.

She rushed up the drive, over to the left, along the bumpy gravel track leading to her cottage, almost running by the time she got near it. Then she turned the key in a rush, opened the creaky door and slammed it shut behind her, dead bolting it for extra security.

The thing with Alan had driven her a bit nuts; she already knew that. And this being her first solo trip in a very long time, possibly forever, had also affected her. But this was crazy, hardly enough cause to start hallucinating!

Back inside the cozy cottage, the entire experience seemed almost comical to her. She let out a nervous chuckle as she put her handbag down on the side table and unbuttoned her coat. Maybe it had been just the stress.

She double-checked all the curtains and switched on every lamp she could find. It wasn't very cold yet, or she would have been tempted to light the fireplace as well.

Now what? Perhaps she should have not been such a coward and actually waited at the edge of the woods to call Lily up properly. It would have been nice to tell her about the lengthy drive across the Scottish Highlands, and of course about Derek. None of that was an option anymore now, not until she headed out towards the village again.

There was no TV in the cottage, just an old HiFi system, the type with an LP player on top. The bookcase that stood beside contained a selection of old records. Clarice read the spines of a random few and selected the first thing she recognized: The Beatles, and placed it on top of the deck with trembling fingers. As the first guitar chords started to play, she felt herself relax.

Too bad she hadn't picked up a bottle of wine from that little shop. Perhaps she would drive back there in the morning...

Exhausted after her eventful first day in Scotland, she settled into the large armchair facing the empty fireplace and closed her eyes. The music did its best to soothe her. She wasn't hungry after eating the cake earlier, and neither did she have the will or energy to get up and prepare dinner.

Tomorrow was going to be another day, and she had to be ready to make the most of it. Four-thousand words at least, if not more. This was a sprint as well as a marathon; that's why she was here. She had two weeks to finish her book, or her publisher would drop her, and she couldn't afford for that to happen.

She didn't have time for crazy shadows in the woods, or stories of bear sightings in places where bears shouldn't even exist.

It didn't take long for sleep to overwhelm her, as she sat in that comfortable chair. Even after the LP had stopped playing, and the music had made way for complete silence, she still didn't stir.

That's where she stayed until the morning.

CHAPTER FOUR

That had been a very close call, Derek thought to himself. He couldn't shake the emotional confusion he'd felt after coming face-to-face with Clarice for the first time, so after finishing up in the barn, he'd decided to go for a quick walk.

He had to release tension, to blow off steam. There was no better way to do that than to shift and let his animal side take over for a while. In order to ensure her safety, he made sure that he was well away from the farm before taking off his clothes and hiding them in some fallen leaves in among the trees. Then he closed his eyes and focused.

It didn't take much. Shape-shifting was easier when you were already riled up about something. He felt a tickle pass over his spine, which then traveled down his arms and legs. He watched as his formerly relatively smooth limbs sprouted thick brown fur.

Shifting always started from the core outward. His torso would change first, and then a split second later his head, arms and legs would follow until he had transformed completely into a brown bear.

Derek planned to go for a bit of an outing, head towards his favorite stream for an evening snack of raw fish perhaps. What he wanted the most was to get away from the farm for a while, so that there was no risk of picking up Clarice's tempting scent, which he knew would whip his hormones into even more of a frenzy.

Only, things didn't turn out quite how he had planned.

Once he had shifted and started running towards the

stream that lay about halfway between the farmhouse and the nearby village, he couldn't clear his mind of all the thoughts and urges Clarice had stirred up. In bear form, he was even more susceptible to the attraction he'd felt toward her.

The sights and smells of the woods did nothing to distract him. He could even still pick up her perfume, despite being almost a mile away from the farm.

Once at the stream, all he could do was listlessly watch the fish as they struggled to jump up the fast currents. He didn't feel like reaching out and catching one. He didn't even want to cool his paws in the icy waters as he normally would have.

None of it held much interest for him. Instead, Clarice's scent kept making its way into his nostrils, beckoning him to turn around and seek her out.

He left the stream and didn't walk as much as drag his paws on the way back to the farm. His entire being was spurring him on to run to her, but he did his best to resist. He thoughtlessly wandered on, carving a path through the empty landscape that ran parallel to the road.

For the first time in all the years he'd spent on his own, he wished for someone to talk to. He had to figure out why he was so affected by a human, of all things. He'd read of bears who had gotten so used to their animal form that they'd sought out the company of actual bears over their own kind, but never did he hear of anyone mating outside their species.

To take a human mate was wrong, wasn't it? How would it even work, when the bears' code of secrecy insisted that humans should never find out about their existence? If she found out the truth about him, it would endanger his entire kind. Humans were afraid of what they didn't understand. If he tried to pursue her without telling her the truth, that would be equally wrong.

And yet, he couldn't help how he felt about her.

His brooding thoughts were interrupted by a fresh waft of her scent accompanied by footsteps against gravel. *Clarice.*

Across his entire body, his fur stood up to attention, as if he was readying for a fight. He paused and got up on his hind legs, standing as still as he possibly could while observing her.

What was she doing here?

He watched as she walked along the road, clumsily stumbling over a particularly rough patch of gravel, until she recovered herself, phone in hand.

When she reached the edge of the woods, she paused and looked around, raising her phone into the air and waving it around ahead of her. Finally, she let out a triumphant 'Aha!' and smiled, placing the phone back into her purse.

Derek didn't have a cell phone, only a land line, which nobody ever called except telemarketers and tourists hoping to book a vacation. Still, he'd heard visitors say that most mobile providers didn't cover his farm. Most tourists didn't mind, but it seemed Clarice had had a pressing need to contact someone. A boyfriend perhaps?

The thought angered him.

His jaw tensed, and his upper lip curled instinctively into a snarl.

He decided to turn around and leave before he was spotted, though just as he got down on all fours again, Clarice turned as well and let out a fearful gasp. He hadn't been able to pick up on her physiology before, she was too far away, but now that she was startled, her bodily responses were loud enough for his sensitive hearing to pick up. Her heartbeat had sped up into a frantic pace.

Shit. She had spotted him.

Both froze, Clarice with her arms wrapped around herself, and Derek partially hidden behind one of the thicker trees in this part of the woods. Seconds passed as she continued to look in his direction, and then her breaths as well as her heartbeat relaxed, and she started to walk back to where she had come from before: the farm.

He breathed a sigh of relief as well, then made his way deeper into the woods, taking care to only walk on those extra mossy patches on the ground so that he didn't make any noise. Once again, a very close call.

That was it. He had to resort to desperate measures if he was going to remain sane throughout her stay. He left her to walk back to her cottage on her own and ran.

As fast as his paws could carry him, he pushed on until he had made it to the edge of his territory. There he let out an almighty roar, calling out for whoever was listening. Bears were territorial, so his call was bound to be noticed.

———◆———

"Derek," a calm, if slightly cold female voice called out to him, almost an hour after he had reached the no-man's-land that lay between his and his closest neighbors' lands. Elise - his older cousin from his mother's side - had come to answer his call.

He nodded and waited patiently as the female approached. The light brown bear that emerged from the shrubbery surrounding his meeting place of choice eyed him suspiciously.

"What brings you here?" Elise asked.

"This is going to be awkward, but I was hoping for some insights." Derek straightened himself in an attempt to appear rather more confident than he felt. It was a massive hit to his pride, coming here for advice, but even though they hadn't been close ever since he'd taken over the farm, Elise was still family. He didn't know who else to turn to. "As you know, other bears are hard to find nowadays. I was wondering if you could share some information, for old times' sake."

"What about?" Elise asked.

"Uhh... it's rather delicate."

"Just spit it out, Derek."

"When you and Jack got together, it was fate, wasn't it?"

The female bear cocked her head to the side and simply stared at him.

"Was it?" Derek pushed again.

"I wouldn't say *fate,* but I knew immediately what was going on."

"I don't understand, the way Mum used to talk about what happened between Dad and her, she said it was their destiny to pair up."

"Your mother always was the romantic sort. No, I'm convinced it's biology, pure and simple. We pick our mates according to who is most compatible biologically. It's nature at work; that's all."

"But it only happens once in a lifetime?" Derek asked.

"Again, it's in our best interests to mate for life, to ensure the survival of our cubs. Once we pair up, our brains release certain hormones to ensure we remain faithful to that one significant other."

"Right." Derek paused for a moment, uncertain about how to ask the most pressing question on his mind. "So it's all to do with producing healthy offspring, correct? Which means this sort of thing could only happen with another bear..."

"What are you suggesting? You've developed a crush

on a wolf or something?" Elise curled her lips, revealing a row of perfectly white sharp teeth in something somewhere between a smile and a sneer. The rivalry between wolves and bears ran deep, so it wasn't surprising for her to tease him like that.

"Not exactly."

Elise observed him in silence, which made him even more uneasy.

"Have you ever heard of a bear choosing a human mate?" he asked at last. As awkward as the situation was, he really did need to know. And there wasn't another bear to ask for many miles.

"A human..." Elise sat down in the damp heather, seemingly lost in thought. "Apparently in the cities, inter-species dating is a lot more common than it used to be. The challenges are many, though. It only works for those who have chosen to live fully in the human world and lost their bear side. However, now I'm reminded of another story from a long time ago - it's more of a myth than anything else. Did your mother ever tell you of Bhaltair and Aileen?"

She looked up, her eyes locking with Derek's, and her expression once again grave and serious after the werewolf remark, which had been partially in jest.

He slowly shook his head, the names did seem familiar, but he did not recall the story at all.

"In the olden days," Elise began, "back when we lived openly among humans, once every few generations, a bear would discover his true mate in a human. My speculation is, it's to do with revitalizing the bloodline. As the story goes, Bhaltair was the leader of his clan, a bachelor well into adulthood, who despite being surrounded by women of his kind never bonded with any of them. One day upon visiting a nearby village, he came across a human girl,

Aileen, and it was as if lightning struck. His inner bear knew, he knew, he had to take her as his mate. Of course, Bhaltair, being a clan leader and accustomed to being in charge wasn't subtle about the matter, and some say that there had been hostilities between his clan and the humans already. It was more of an abduction than a love story in the end..."

"Oh?" Derek could barely hide his shock at hearing Elise describe pretty much what he'd felt when he first saw Clarice. *Lightning.*

"When Aileen's father, Lord Domnall, found out where she'd been taken, he collected as many men as he could, calling them in from the surrounding villages. It inspired one of the greatest genocides in our history. You will have heard of the *Sons of Domnall...* It is said they evolved from that very first group of soldiers, who vowed to hunt us to extinction."

"And that's why we keep our existence a secret," Derek remarked, finally remembering bits and pieces of a similar story his mother had told him a very long time ago.

"Perhaps. Or perhaps it's just a bedtime story we tell our cubs. A morality tale aimed to illustrate why the code of secrecy is so important. Any particular reason you're coming to me with all this?" Elise asked.

"I was just curious, didn't know who else to ask... As you know, Aidan's turned into quite the globetrotter, so you're the only family around." Derek brushed away her question.

"I see. Well then, glad to be of help."

Derek nodded at Elise, who understood that this signaled the end of their little chat. She turned back one last time, no doubt wondering what he had gotten himself into, then ran off North, where undoubtedly Jack would be waiting for her at home.

It wasn't what he had wanted to hear, especially her mention of the *Sons of Domnall* was very worrying, but at least he now knew his situation wasn't unique.

Although his mother had been a firm believer in following your destiny - especially when it came to mates - Derek was a lot more practical. He wasn't about to leave his reality in favor of a human existence. His inner bear wouldn't allow it anyway, it practically tried to claw its way to the surface every time he got near Clarice. No, he refused to jump head first to his doom.

Elise's story suggested that Aileen hadn't felt the same connection with Bhaltair. Humans must be incapable of sensing these things as bears do. Chances were, his own lightning strike with Clarice was equally one-sided.

Then there was the code of secrecy to consider. It existed for a reason, and not just to hide from the mythical bear assassin squad, the *Sons of Domnall*. Those guys were probably a figment of bear imagination, but that didn't detract from the fact that people were scared of what they didn't understand, and scared people were dangerous. Even if Clarice did feel an attraction for him, he couldn't trust her with the secret of his species.

He was going to fight this thing tooth and nail. It was only two weeks, for God's sake. Surely he could resist his urges long enough to watch Clarice drive off in that rented hatchback of hers, never to return...

CHAPTER FIVE

Indeed, the next morning brought a brand new day for Clarice. She was up bright and early by seven, made herself a hearty breakfast and settled down on the comfortable armchair by the fireplace with her laptop. It wasn't ideal, writing in an armchair, but she couldn't resist its inviting plushness and the feel of its velvety material against her skin.

Before everything went south with Alan, Clarice had already prepared an outline for her latest novel and written the first three chapters. Everything from the fourth chapter on though was as good as useless. The moment she'd caught Alan red-handed, she couldn't get into the mood to write the sweet historical romance she had set out to write, and instead found that her characters grew minds of their own.

Chapter after chapter consisted of the hero and heroine arguing, their antics escalating drastically with each sentence. By the end, she was in a good mood to kill off both of them.

That's not a romance, Clarice said to herself while re-reading it all. She might as well have missed her deadline entirely if she was going to submit something this inappropriate.

With a few clicks on her touchpad, she got rid of all of the offending words and was once again faced with a blank page at chapter four.

Think happy, romantic thoughts.

Instead of the blond well-polished and svelte hero of her outline, she kept thinking back to Derek's imposing physique. The face of her romantic fantasies wasn't clean-shaven as she originally imagined but featured a scruffy, extremely masculine beard and brown hair.

Screw it.

Clarice picked up her notebook, the one she was accustomed to recording early thoughts and book ideas in, flipped it open and started to brainstorm. After writing frantically for the better part of an hour, she had a new character profile and plot outline ready.

Her heroine, Lady Adlington wasn't going to fall head over heels in love with the Duke of Harringate as initially imagined. No, she would have an illicit affair with the brusque stable hand in the Duke's employ. When the relationship inevitably came to light, it created a huge scandal. It caused the two lovers to go on the run, to find a place where they could live their lives undisturbed, away from the strict class divide of Victorian England that sought to end their romance. Perfect.

She put the notes down and picked up the laptop again, going through the first three chapters to make the necessary changes. Most of it still fit. After adding in the odd hint here and there, as well as a scene when Lady Adlington first laid eyes on the handsome man of her dreams, Clarice's fingers seemed to fly over the keys at an incredible speed.

This place had worked out amazingly well for Clarice. Gone was the anguish over her failed relationship that had stood in her way back home. No longer did everything feel hopeless, because in her heart Clarice had felt all love was doomed to fail.

She had found her inspiration again. Her muse came in the unlikely form of a married farmer with rough, strong hands and broad shoulders. A man who probably had never opened up a romance novel or thought much about emotions in general. A man so unavailable, Clarice couldn't help but be attracted to him like a moth to a flame.

———•◆•———

It was already dark by the time Clarice put down the laptop. She'd forgotten to eat or drink anything. She'd even failed to get up and stretch at regular intervals, and as such her day of laser focused writing had taken a toll on her.

After a cup of tea, she felt some of her senses return to her, but her body was still tied up in knots. A walk, that's what she needed.

She stretched her arms, her legs, even tried to untangle her spine, and picked up her coat to head outside. As she opened the front door, she noticed a parcel wrapped in newspaper waiting for her on top of the welcome mat outside.

After picking it up, she weighed it in her hands. It was heavy, despite its rather small size.

Back indoors, she placed it on the small round dining table and started unwrapping the various layers of paper. Inside she found a plain piece of paper with a note, resting on top of what looked like a big fish fillet covered in cling film.

Freshly caught this morning. Don't leave it too long.

The note wasn't signed, but it was obvious that it had come from the farmer and his wife. Probably more from his wife, Derek himself didn't seem like the sort of guy who went around randomly gifting people food. Still, the gesture made her smile, and immediately her stomach rumbled to remind her that indeed, she hadn't eaten all day.

If only she knew how to cook, or at least had a connection on her phone which would allow her to consult Google for instructions.

Flipping the note over, she saw that there was yet more writing on the back. A recipe. *How thoughtful.*

After leaving the parcel in the modest fridge underneath the counter, she once again stepped out of the cottage for a short wander around the farm. No way was she going to risk her sanity as well as safety by leaving the property in the dark. She had thoroughly learned her lesson the previous evening.

She wandered down the gravel track towards the driveway leading up to the main house and for the first time since arriving on McMillan Farm, she allowed herself a good look at the building. It looked old, at least 100 years, if not more. The pitched roof suggested the farmhouse was very spacious inside, which seemed unusual for a utilitarian building of that age.

The barns surrounding the house stood in a grouping of three, around a main courtyard facing towards the other side of the driveway. There was a stable set further back, but no sign of any animals, perhaps they were still out grazing.

She walked along the side of the house, taking care that nobody was watching her. Although she didn't want to seem sneaky, she really didn't want to be forced into any polite conversations with anyone, least of all Derek, the sexy farmer.

The net curtains on towards the left of the building barely concealed the dim lighting inside. Perhaps they were just sitting down for dinner, the man and his wife.

Clarice walked on along the path through the partially wilted summer flowerbeds planted along the main wall either side of the large front door. Once she'd reached the corner, she noticed that this side of the house featured a well-manicured kitchen garden, with vines climbing neatly erected poles. She wasn't sure what they were growing there; she'd never had much of a green thumb herself, but it sure looked pretty as well as useful.

Further along the side of the house was a small fenced off area containing a few chickens that were surprisingly quiet. Perhaps they had already fallen asleep in their coop for the night.

Before she had much of a chance to explore further, did a light switch on inside the room looking out over the kitchen garden. This window didn't have any curtains, allowing her a clear peek inside. She could see Derek's silhouette walk into the room that turned out to contain a dining area, carrying a large tray. Yep, they were getting ready to eat.

Outside in the darkness, Clarice was reasonably certain she wouldn't be seen, at least not as long as the light was on indoors, but she didn't want to take any unnecessary risks.

After observing the man as he sat down at the rustic wooden table in the center of the room, and waiting for a moment to see if his wife would follow - she was nowhere to be seen - Clarice quietly traced her steps back to where she'd come from. Around the side of the house, crossing the lawn in front of the main facade back to the driveway that led to the gravel track. She took care to step only on the grass, not on the gravel so that her footsteps wouldn't make much noise.

It occurred to her that there was something odd about this farm, something missing. Not only was it weird that she'd never once seen the farmer's wife, that wasn't all that piqued her suspicion: they didn't have a dog. Didn't almost everyone in the country keep at least one watch dog?

Weird.

How would they know if anyone intruded onto their land? Cameras? No, the farmer didn't seem like the techy kind. She shrugged to herself and tried to stop her imagination from running away with her again. Perhaps they just didn't like dogs...

Clarice took one last breath of the earthy, cool air outside her cottage, then stepped back indoors and undid her coat. Time to tackle that fish, for better or for worse. She didn't have anything else to eat besides bread and eggs, and those could get tedious after a while.

———◆———

Day after day passed in largely the same fashion. She got up early to do her work, and her focus was never broken until hours later when she felt her body revolt to the crazy work ethic she'd developed.

Her novel was progressing nicely, and the story turned out to be much more captivating than that first outline she'd prepared months ago. She was certain her editor was going to love it. The drama was intense, the romance palpable, and the characters seemed so real to her that they could very well just walk off the page as actual people. It was magical, how she'd found joy in writing again, when previous attempts the last months had felt more like pulling teeth.

Life at Moss Cottage seemed easy otherwise also. Every day a new treat ended up on her welcome mat, which she gratefully accepted. Often it was something sweet, but occasionally it was a piece of meat or fish, as well as fresh vegetables that undoubtedly had been grown in the kitchen garden. In case of the latter, there was always a brief note attached with a recipe on the back.

She made it a point to thank Derek - and pass on the message to his wife - whenever she had the opportunity to speak with him, which wasn't often. He seemed to be a very industrious man, always busy, always working.

Although she'd tried to put a stop to her wandering thoughts, every time she saw him, whether close enough to talk to, or hard at work further away from her cottage, her desire for him grew.

Every time she actually saw Derek during the day, she couldn't shake the feeling that they'd formed some kind of connection, a magnetic bond of some sort. Of course she knew that it was all one-sided, that desperation and perhaps loneliness had colored her perception.

The more she yearned for Derek's attention, the better the progress on her novel.

He visited her in her dreams in the mornings, before she was properly awake. It was during those hours that he whispered the words into her ear that the hero of her novel - Lady Adlington's unexpected lover - would say to melt her heart.

Meanwhile, the man himself had shown no indication whatsoever that he felt any attraction towards her. His routine never wavered. Even when he was doing chores around the cottages, repairing a fence, or trimming the hedges, he showed no interest in what she was up to. He never came by for a chat, and the occasional exchanges between the two seemed to irritate him rather than give him enjoyment.

In the evenings, when Derek had retreated inside the main house, Clarice continued her short walks around the farm. Although she'd tried to be stealthy - though not in a creepy stalker sort of way - she did at times feel like she was being watched. Either way, her walks were the only thing keeping her back from locking up after largely sedentary days, so she wasn't going to give them up no matter what. And part of her kept hoping she could catch a glimpse of Derek's wife.

She wasn't sure what she was hoping to see. Worthy competition? A confirmation that she stood no chance at all? Perhaps she wished most of all to see Derek's wife as a kind person deserving of his loyalty so that finally she could stop obsessing about the man. But his wife never left the house as far as she could tell.

Clarice never once laid eyes on her.

CHAPTER SIX

One afternoon, a week after her first arrival at McMillan Farm, Clarice was already coming up to the final climax of the novel. It was crazy to think that she'd achieved so much in so little time, but she knew the work had taken its toll on her.

She decided to take a break while it was still light out. A chance to let her sore muscles relax, while drinking in the beautiful surroundings of her rural retreat. Once she put her head down and started to write, she might not be able to resurface until the resolution to her fictional couple's troubles had presented itself, and by then it would be too late to head out.

Plus, she'd run out of cookies and eggs, necessitating a trip to restock. The skies overhead were grey as ever when she stepped out of the cottage, and the wind rustled against the remaining leaves on the trees all round.

Fortunately, because Clarice had access to her rental car, the weather did not worry her. Walking might have been healthier, but the village with its tiny store was so far off, it would be less of a walk and more of a hike to get there and back.

She was slightly disappointed that she didn't see Derek anywhere on her way out the main gates, but then just focused on the drive ahead. Her car whirled up fallen leaves from the road. The trees had turned color completely during the short stay at McMillan Farm. Clarice took note of the shades of red and orange she saw, determined to embellish some of the descriptions in her novel with details of the same.

Clarice even wound down the window to allow the brisk, damp autumn air into the car. It smelled earthy, rich, and it was cold enough to prickle against her skin. By all accounts, it was a beautiful day in its own right, despite the sun not being anywhere in sight.

As she came up to the turn that headed out of the wooded patch around the farm, she remembered how about a week ago, this was where she had come to send that message to Lily. She ought to phone her from the village just to give her an update on what was going on. Should she mention Derek? Why the hell not? Perhaps Lily could talk some sense into her.

The road wound on through the heather covered landscape. Over smaller as well as bigger hillocks, over the occasional cattle grill dividing up the asphalt. She passed by fields with grazing sheep, which were one of the few reminders that this place was actually inhabited.

Clarice told herself that as soon as she'd finish her book, she would take a day or so to explore the island some more. Perhaps with the help of her satellite navigation, she would be able to find a road leading directly to the coast. If the distant views were anything to go by, a close-up of the shoreline should be breathtaking.

Darker clouds rolled in over the taller hills in the distance, but before the weather turned for the worse, Clarice could see the first houses at the edge of the village up ahead. She was almost there.

Minutes later, she parked up beside the house with the daily needs shop. The door was open just like last time. She set off an automatic bell as she entered.

"Afternoon," the old man's voice greeted Clarice from across the room, where he sat at his table with a newspaper.

"Hello!" She smiled widely at him, glad for the

interaction, however short. "Just hoping to restock on a few things."

"Of course. Please help yourself."

Clarice walked through the aisles, picking up mostly the same items she'd bought only a week earlier. Cookies, eggs, bread, as well as the only bottle of red wine she could find in the entire store. She would use the latter as a reward for when she finished the book.

Coming up closer to the table where the old man waited, she spied a rack of greeting cards, where she paused for a moment. A souvenir of this place would be nice indeed. She picked out a particularly scenic shot of the rugged cliffs that rose up from the center of the Isle of Skye. Once she got her hands on a first copy of this novel she'd been working on, she planned to keep the card inside it, as a reminder of her time here.

A better reminder, of course, would be a picture of Derek, her main inspiration, but she didn't think she could muster the courage to ask him if she could take one.

"Are you able to find everything you need?" asked the old man while looking up from his newspaper.

"Yes. All done." Clarice wandered over towards him, placing her various purchases on the table. She waited while he added everything up on his little notepad, just like he'd done the last time she was here. If she didn't start a conversation soon, she would lose the opportunity. Yet she wasn't sure how to begin, nervous that he would see right through her and guess her intentions.

"So... The weather seems to be taking a turn for the worse today," Clarice began.

The old man nodded. "A storm's coming in from the East; looks to be a bad'un." He handed her the note after finishing his calculations. "So how have you been enjoying your stay at the cottage?"

"It's very nice. A real quiet getaway. Just what the doctor ordered," Clarice said. This was her chance.

"And what lovely people. Baking cakes, and whatnot leaving it outside my door.

The old man cocked his head to the side, his grayish-blue eyes fixed on Clarice's face.

"Derek McMillan does take pride in his produce," he remarked.

"Mhmm," Clarice agreed.

"What *people* do you refer to? Has his brother, Aidan turned up? I haven't seen him about in a while," the man remarked.

"You mean, it's just him living there? I assumed..." Clarice couldn't hide her shock. "The cakes and everything..."

There was an awkward silence between the two.

"You thought he was married," he said finally.

"Well... Yes!"

The old man let out a laugh. "He doesn't seem like the baking type, true, but I've been lucky enough to taste some of his creations at the annual village fete. McMillan has hidden talents."

Clarice remained quiet. What a strange man, to never correct her once when she mentioned his non-existent wife. It hurt because it clearly signaled that he'd preferred keep up with her mistaken assumption, if it made him seem unavailable. He must really dislike her.

She picked up the paper bag of groceries and forced a smile while avoiding eye contact.

"Well, I'd better be off then, before the storm hits."

"That would be wise," the shopkeeper said. "Bye now. Drive safe."

"Bye." She turned, just a little too eagerly, her eyes glazing over slightly despite her best efforts to keep her emotions in check.

Shit. She knew most guys wouldn't consider her a catch. She wasn't skinny, glamorous, or even particularly exciting company due to her introverted nature. But to find out that someone found her so repulsive that he wouldn't even correct her about the whole wife assumption, in an attempt to keep his distance from her? That was a new low.

It was the icing on the poisoned cake. A new blow to her self-worth that almost stung worse than Alan's unfaithfulness. She had been mostly indifferent about Alan up to that point. She was far from indifferent when it came to Derek.

She carelessly dumped the groceries onto the passenger seat of the car and took her place behind the wheel. What a mess. She had to get away from here, to get out of the village, and far away from potentially prying eyes before the waterworks began.

Still shocked, she turned the car around and slammed her foot down, speeding back up the road where she had just come from. Tears clouded her vision as she navigated largely on autopilot. Around the blind bends, over the cattle grill, which made a hell of a noise underneath her tires. The only thing louder was the rumble of thunder overhead.

The sky might as well been falling. Her headlights turned on automatically as the dark clouds gathered above the car. The weather was a perfect reflection of her mood. She felt humiliated and deeply hurt in what little remained of her pride. She wanted to scream. Instead she hit the steering with her fists a few times, then cried at the hopelessness of it all.

The worst part was, the whole thing with Derek, whatever she felt, it was just a stupid infatuation. She didn't even know the man. All she knew was that he was tall, broad, and had a certain rugged, masculine charm that had drawn her to him involuntarily.

She didn't know the first thing going on in his head - if anything actually did happen in there - except that he clearly had developed some kind of instinctive dislike for her. There was no other explanation.

The winds started lashing against the car, making it feel slightly imbalanced. She felt more pressure on the steering, forcing her to correct against the stormy gusts aiming to push her off the road.

She didn't need this. After all the shit with Alan that threatened to ruin her career as a writer, as well as her sanity as a person, she really didn't deserve to be kicked back down when she'd finally found her bearings again. How was she going to finish the book now? How was she going to find a resolution for her imaginary couple, when her muse had all but betrayed her?

Although she wasn't sure how she would react if she saw Derek now, she had nowhere else to go but back to the cottage. Chances were, he wouldn't be around anyway. He rarely was at this time of day.

Tears were streaming down her face now, silently. She'd stopped sobbing.

The landscape that had looked so pretty in the misty conditions from before now seemed hostile as well as bleak. She was relieved to see the woods up ahead. Soon she'd be back, and she'd lock herself inside the cottage and perhaps open that bottle of wine a few days earlier than planned. Or she would make some tea, better yet, she'd make a hot chocolate using the cocoa powder she'd found in one of the kitchen cupboards.

Only, the weather had other ideas for her. As soon as she made it into the dark wooded patch surrounding the farm, a bright flash of lighting followed instantly by a loud thunder crack startled her, making her jerk the steering. The car skidded onto a patch of wet leaves. A split second later, one of the trees that had stood proud and healthy moments before, split and started to lean over dangerously across the road ahead.

She had no way of stopping, no opportunity to avoid it. The charred trunk was falling too close to the front of the car, and she was going too fast to be able to react. A jarring crash later, did both the car and the felled tree come to an abrupt halt together.

Her vision blurred, details of trees and brown, wet leaves making way for nothing but a bright, loud white. Then the darkness took over.

CHAPTER SEVEN

Although it pained him, Derek knew that his efforts to stay far away from Clarice were in both their best interests. Every day he had tried to limit his activities near the cottage to times when he knew she'd be working inside, and he wouldn't risk running into her.

The thing about running a farm alone was that there was always something to do. The work never finished, so he could keep himself occupied as far away from her as possible whenever the need arose.

The one thing he hadn't been able to stop himself from doing was leaving her treats.

His evenings at the house consisted of stockpiling supplies to prepare for winter. He was doing his best to harvest all he could before the kitchen garden would inevitably stop producing. Whatever he didn't eat straightaway, he preserved.

Still, he couldn't resist using some of his existing supplies - especially sweet ones - to produce the occasional cake or other treat. Not for himself, though he had always had a sweet tooth, but for her.

His keen sense of smell told him that without his intervention, the woman ate eggs for dinner every day, which was something he could not accept. Whenever he went fishing, he caught a little extra for her, when he planned to eat lamb for dinner, he shared his ingredients with her.

She always thanked him profusely, or rather, thanked his imaginary wife - same thing - so he was certain that she did appreciate the gifts.

And she didn't seem like one of those neurotic diet nuts, the ones who read the labels of whatever they eat, and seemed to revel in denying themselves any pleasure from food. No, Clarice was more of a hedonist, someone who allowed themselves to smell the roses - or eat the chocolate in this case. He appreciated that about her.

But despite his best efforts, things had changed over the past week. No longer was his attraction towards her largely shallow, inspired by the odd glimpse or scent. Even when he had his back turned towards her, it was as if he could see her more clearly than when he was actually looking at her.

Derek couldn't explain it without making comparisons to the stories his mother used to tell him. When bears found their mate, the one that fate - or biology, as Elise had put it - had in mind for them, they connected on a deep, subconscious level. They started to share a kind of understanding that didn't require words to communicate.

Empathy as a term didn't quite cover what happened to bears and their soul mates. And if this wasn't happening to him now, he would have never even believed it was possible for a bond to run so deeply.

When he walked past Moss Cottage, he could sense what Clarice was up to. If her work was going well or if she was pondering something. It wasn't clear, he wasn't a mind reader, but he always had some idea of her mood. In the evenings when she went for her short walks, he knew where she was without fail. He could pinpoint her position accurately, without even looking out the window.

In the old stories, these strange feelings and bonds were always mutual, but in his case, they couldn't be. She was human. There was no way that she could sense things as keenly as he did. The story Elise had told him confirmed this, plus Clarice hadn't acted like she felt anything but unease for him.

He tried to keep his thoughts about her to a minimum, to stay away from what-ifs and speculations on what might have been if she'd also been a bear and not a human. Instead, he'd marked the date of her departure in his calendar in bright red, and counted the days leading up to it with keen anticipation as well as dread.

Today, they had crossed the half-way point between her arrival and impending departure. It was a relief that he'd gotten this far without doing anything stupid, but also a worry that in just a week, he'd connected so deeply with her. There was no way of predicting how much stronger her pull on him would get before she left.

She'd worked as usual for most of the morning, then abruptly taken a break and gone out. He could hear her car start, and the crunch of gravel under her tires while he tidied up the raised beds in the kitchen garden. She was happy, almost triumphant as she left, and Derek caught himself whistling as he worked as a result.

Only when she was gone, did he realize how distracting her presence on the farm had been. He hadn't even noticed the dark clouds and the electricity building in the air. Bad weather was coming, and it had completely caught him by surprise.

He scanned the darkening skies, then hurriedly put away his tools and headed indoors. The radio confirmed his suspicions; the weather was going to deteriorate quite a bit, and the Met Office had even put out an amber alert.

Hopefully, Clarice would be back by the time the storm hit. Weather could get dangerous on the island, and they were predicting gusts strong enough to cause quite a bit of damage.

As he waited, he reorganized the stack of wood beside the fireplace. If the predictions were accurate, temperatures would plummet. Once he'd finished that, he headed into the kitchen to put on a pot of stew.

If he wanted to stay alert, he had to make sure there'd be plenty of warmth and nourishment available to him, or the urge to hibernate would threaten to overwhelm his senses. Hibernation was something he wasn't willing to risk with a visitor on the farm.

Just as the large pot started to simmer on the stove, and Derek had the chance to sit on one of the heavy dining chairs, did a feeling of unease start to pluck at his thoughts. The rain started to lash down against the windows, and the winds were whistling in the trees surrounding the farmhouse.

Surely, she couldn't have gone far? She would have just driven to the village, probably to visit the modest shop there. But he didn't sense her anywhere nearby yet, so she was still out of his range.

His discomfort grew until his instincts were almost screaming at him that something was going terribly wrong. Finally, he could no longer fight it. He put on a warm, waterproof coat and left the house to investigate.

For a moment, he paused near in front of the barn containing his trusty old Landrover. No, the route through the forest would be quicker, as well as more sheltered from the elements. His feet carried him forward almost involuntarily, and by the time he made it through the farm gates, he was sprinting.

He'd barely crossed the first tree-covered hill that lay between him and the open heathland nearer the village when a sharp pain pierced his chest. This was no longer a merely hypothetical worry that had inspired him to leave the house and brave the storm. He could feel the danger, the pain Clarice was in with as much clarity as he could feel the rain hitting his face.

Despite being fully clothed, he didn't stop to undress but shifted instantly. The winds were battering against the trees with so much intensity, it drowned out the sound of ripping fabric as his once smooth human torso sprouted thick brown fur and ripped its way through the much too small jacket. Everything he had worn only moments earlier was left in tatters on the wet, moss-covered ground underneath.

Up ahead, dim lights filtered through the trees and dense rainfall. As he approached the scene, he could see that it was indeed Clarice's gray hatchback. One of the first things he noticed was the smell of burnt wood, originating from a tree that had split in two across the base, causing the top end of it to fall into the road. The second thing was... blood.

His heart sank. There were no cries of pain, no noises at all coming from the car itself, just the incessant drum rolls of heavy rain, hitting the roof. Inside, Clarice slumped forward, her head resting on a blood-stained airbag. Of course, he feared the worst. She wasn't moving, and he couldn't hear her vital signs through the howling winds surrounding them.

He grabbed at the handle, but the car door wouldn't budge, so he rushed to the passenger side of the car and broke the window with a powerful blow from his paw. The glass shattered into a million little pieces, covering the seat inside, some of it landing in Clarice's hair. He grabbed at the rim of the door, and a strong tug later, threw the twisted remnants of it into the shrubbery behind him.

It didn't matter to him anymore that he risked discovery, that if Clarice was, in fact, fine, she could open her eyes at any moment and come face-to-face with a huge brown bear. He couldn't just leave her here, stuck inside this tin box. The road to McMillan Farm was secluded and lonely at the best of times. The nearest help was the voluntary fire brigade based in Portree, forty minutes away, and during a storm like this, there was no chance of them arriving anytime soon.

Whatever had to be done was up to Derek, and Derek alone.

He climbed into the car, his massive weight causing the suspension to creak dangerously. Although he could reach Clarice with his snout, he was too big to fit in far enough to get her out. At least from here he could hear her heartbeat. She was alive, but who knew for how long if she stayed here.

With one surprisingly accurate tap of his claw, he managed to undo the buckle of her seatbelt. He reached out and gently pushed her back into her seat, and then aimed the next blow at the airbag, tearing it free from the steering wheel to give him more of a view of what was going on.

She seemed to be in one piece though there was an ugly gash on her forehead with blood dripping from it. Her breaths were slow, calm, but not weak. Despite everything, she was still the most beautiful woman he'd ever seen.

Still, she wasn't conscious, so there was no way of finding out if that bump on her head was her only injury.

With so many unknowns, and the bad weather continuing, Derek didn't have time to carefully deliberate his next move. He closed his eyes and focused on his human form, feeling his limbs contract back to their original shape.

Taking advantage of his much more dexterous fingers, he freed Clarice of the seatbelt completely, then checked that both her legs were free underneath the steering wheel. He carefully levered her out of her seat, over the gear knob and into the passenger seat. Then he got out of the car completely, and with one arm supporting her shoulders, the other running through the crook of her knees, he lifted her up towards freedom.

She was still limp, completely out of it, which was just as well because the situation looked bad. His clothes were lying in tatters somewhere in the woods, and he preferred not to have to explain his current nudity to her.

There was no doctor nearby, and the storm was far from over. The cold rain started to chill his naked skin, and Clarice didn't have much warmth in her either. The nearest clinic was halfway across the island, and if the storm didn't get them on the way, the cold temperatures surely would. There was nothing else he could do but carry her home and hope that she'd wake up on her own. He had to trust that she would be fine without immediate medical attention.

He started walking back up the same way through the trees as he had come earlier. But in his human form, without the protective thick fur, the cold significantly slowed his progress. Derek could feel his muscles tighten and lethargy wash over him.

He looked down at Clarice's face. She was completely still, even as the heavy droplets hit her ivory skin. It took all the energy he had left to transform yet again, taking the utmost care that the claws his hands sprouted didn't hurt her. Once again covered in warm fur, he started on the walk home.

Running on all fours would have been quicker and more comfortable for him, but as long as Clarice was protected against the elements in his strong arms, slow and steady would have to do. He kept going, zig-zagging through the woods while hunching over just enough to keep her dry.

By the time they got back to the farmhouse together, her cheeks had even warmed to a rosy pink. If he didn't know any better, he might have thought she was sleeping.

CHAPTER EIGHT

Clarice had the strangest dream.

After crashing her car into the tree - or having the tree crash into her, she wasn't certain how it had happened exactly, she'd been trapped in a world of white noise. She couldn't move, couldn't scream, couldn't even feel her body.

Somehow, she had made it out of the wreck and back to the cottage, though. She had been aware of her movements, somewhat, as well as the noises around her, but she hadn't been able to see much of what had occurred. The one thing that stood out to her was Derek's voice. He'd asked if she was okay, and if she was in pain. He'd hoped out loud that she hadn't been badly hurt.

Clarice had wanted to tell him that it was fine, that he didn't need to worry himself, but couldn't open her mouth to form the words. She had caught a glimpse of his face looking down at her, before the overwhelming urge to sleep on had dragged her back into the white. Or perhaps all that had also been part of her dream, and it wasn't Derek who had rescued her.

Somewhere between the car wreck and the farmhouse, she was certain that there had been another presence as well.

She had crashed near the spot where she'd first seen that shadow in the woods and was now certain it had been the bear. Throughout her mysterious rescue, the bear had been watching all along, she could feel his eyes on her. At one point, when her eyes refused to open, she thought she could even feel fur, brushing against her cheek.

The strange thing was, even though she knew the bear was there, close to her, she didn't feel like she was in danger at all. She felt completely safe, cared for even.

The feeling still lingered when she finally did open her eyes.

While she was in the white world, time seemed to hold no importance. Upon waking, and struggling with her vision as her eyes adjusted to the light in the strange room she found herself in, Clarice had no way of figuring out how long she'd been unconscious.

There was a flicker of a candle on the heavy wooden dresser in the corner. She tried to lift her head to get a better view of the rest of the room, but a thumping headache prevented her from moving too much. The bed was comfortable and smelled of clean cotton.

Clarice reached upwards, carefully exploring the painful welt on her forehead with her fingertips, before letting her arm drop beside her body, back onto the soft, bouncy mattress. After staring at the black wooden beams holding up the ceiling for a moment, she turned onto her side.

She was definitely sore, and not just on her head, though there didn't seem to be anything else wrong with her that she could tell. The dresser, the huge wardrobe and the equally solid looking door looked very similar to the furniture and decor of Moss Cottage. But this wasn't her bedroom.

After taking a deep breath, and closing her eyes to focus, she lifted herself, bringing her back closer to the headboard of the bed. It was only then that she realized she was not alone. Towards the other side of the bed, in the corner, a figure slept in a wicker armchair.

Although the candle light did not brighten up that part of the room much, she would recognize him anywhere. Derek.

So it hadn't just been a dream. He had rescued her from the car wreck and carried her all the way back to the farm, just like she'd thought. She wondered what else from her dream was true. The bear? It couldn't be, could it?

Her heart was hammering in her chest as she continued to watch him sleep. Was this his bedroom? Perhaps it was one of the other cottages, surely Derek - who as far as she could tell didn't even like her - wouldn't have brought her into his home?

He stirred slightly, readjusting himself against the side of the large chair. Clarice held her breath in an attempt not to make any sound, but next thing she knew, he had opened his eyes. She shouldn't have seen it, considering how little light there was, and yet there they were: two burning amber orbs, looking right at her.

"Uhm," Clarice started, too nervous to formulate proper words.

"How are you feeling?" Derek's deep voice attempted to soothe her, when Clarice remembered why she'd been upset earlier, before the crash.

"How long was I unconscious for?" she asked coolly. She felt torn. Although she realized how ridiculous it was of her to feel so betrayed over what was essentially a detail - one that isn't even any of her business - still, emotions threatened to well up again. Then again, he did rescue her, she should be thankful for that.

Derek sat up straight, his eyes still burning brightly at her. *Weird.*

"It's dark," Clarice mumbled.

"Power's out," Derek explained. He got up and moved in closer to Clarice's bed, keeping his eyes fixed on her. His movements were deliberate, purposeful. He looked like a man on a mission.

Clarice held her breath, but her heartbeat sped up

anyway. As he moved into the candlelight, she could finally see his expression. His eyes looked her over, lingering on her forehead - Clarice wondered if it looked as bad as it felt - then traveled downward, pausing on her lips. He seemed tense, with his lips pressed together tightly, disguising how sensual and full she'd remembered them to be.

Should she say something?

Derek sat on the edge of the mattress beside her and leaned over, gently brushing a lock of her hair out of the way and carefully inspected her injury.

"That was a close call," he mumbled.

His breath tickled her face as he spoke, and Clarice instinctively closed her eyes for just a moment too long. Having Derek this close to her now overloaded her senses. She wanted nothing more but to lean in, just to get a little taste of him. Despite her earlier assumptions, it did seem as though he cared for her. However, she couldn't be sure he cared for her *like that*.

All she could do to stay civil was to focus on her breathing, in and out, to force her body to slow down, when all it wanted was to spin out of control. She opened her eyes again and noted that he was still there right in front of her.

"That tree, it was too close. I couldn't avoid it," Clarice explained though the words seemed unimportant.

"I know."

"You carried me all the way." Although she'd intended for it to be a question, the sentence came out as a statement. Her memories, however muddled, already told her that he had, in fact, done so. He looked strong, with his broad shoulders and thick biceps that ever so slightly fought against the fabric of his shirt, but she'd crashed quite a long way away, and it wouldn't have been easy to carry her for such a distance. How had he managed that?

A hint of a smile played on Derek's lips, and he nodded.

"I couldn't very well leave you there, could I?"

"I suppose not."

This was the most they'd spoken in the entire week that she'd been at McMillan Farm. The familiarity in Derek's expression made Clarice feel like they knew each other a lot better than they did.

"You're not married," Clarice spoke in a whisper, more to herself than to him.

He shook his head, looking away at the crisp white bed sheet.

"Why didn't you say something?" Clarice wondered out loud. The whole situation was bizarre and confusing.

"I didn't think it made a difference. In another week, you'll go home..." Derek left the rest of his thought for Clarice to fill in for herself. So he did like her? He'd only kept the misunderstanding alive to avoid awkwardness when she left?

Her heart beat even faster, and an awkward silence spread through the room. Clarice had a million and one things she wanted to say and not say at the same time. She wanted to wrap her arms around Derek's shoulders and kiss him, to show him somehow that she wouldn't have just packed up and left if he indeed did have feelings for her.

Bizarrely, she could no longer believe that the attraction she felt towards him was just a childish infatuation. She'd had those before, but this... it ran deeper somehow. Not that she had an explanation for it at all.

Only, she didn't get the chance to do any of it, because the unusually large bedroom door flung open without warning, and there he was: the big brown bear she thought she had seen in the woods on her first day. The one that had wormed its way into her confused dream while she was passed out. She let out a shriek, and in a panic crawled backward against the headboard until she could crawl no further.

"What the!" Derek's voice boomed around the room, distracting the bear, whose gaze darted back and forth between Clarice and the edge of the mattress where Derek had just sat.

She looked over at Derek, hoping desperately that this was indeed his bedroom in the main house, and he had stashed a hunting rifle nearby, or at least something - anything - to protect the two of them against the wild animal that had just entered. But he wasn't sitting beside her anymore. Instead, his already imposing form had made way for an even more impressive one. Another bear, standing squarely in the middle of the room, mere feet away from the intruder.

Clarice didn't know what to do, whether to scream or cry, close her eyes and wish the two scary intruders away. Maybe she had never woken up. Maybe this - as well as the preceding conversation with Derek - was all still part of a crazy dream conjured up by her subconscious. A crazy dream turned terrible nightmare.

She started to feel faint, but the overwhelming sense of panic didn't let her consciousness wane again. Faced now with two bears instead of just one, it was only a matter of time before they'd pounce on her, ripping her to shreds with their huge, sharp teeth.

"Aidan. Bad timing," a voice that sounded more like a growl spoke from Derek's direction.

"Well... This is awkward," the other bear seemed to say, with an equally rough, deep voice.

Clarice felt herself calm down a little bit. There was a

voice in the back of her mind, Derek's voice, which told her she was safe. She believed it without question. Now that she was faced with two *talking* bears, it was obvious her mind was just playing with her.

I'm safe.

Her only regret now was that her intimate chat with Derek earlier probably hadn't been real either.

CHAPTER NINE

"A word, please?" Derek said to Aidan, all the while eyeing Clarice, who continued to be stunned into silence.

Aidan nodded, and both the bears exited the bedroom, leaving Clarice behind.

Aidan's timing couldn't have been worse, Derek thought. Throughout his conversation with Clarice, he could tell that she did feel strongly for him. He could sense her mood: a mixture of yearning and affection. Her hormone levels suggested a physical reaction to his presence. He could smell the pheromones in the air. As she looked at him, her pupils dilated, her cheeks turned flush, and her entire body seemed to invite him in.

Although there was nothing practical about it all, he knew he wouldn't have been able to resist her much longer if Aidan hadn't turned up. Something told him that she wouldn't have either.

"She's human," Aidan remarked.

"Yeah, I know."

"She's seen us." Aidan paced around the hallway while transforming back into his human self.

Derek followed suit so that they were both back in their human form and naked. Aidan shook his head in disbelief, then walked off towards what used to be his old room towards the back of the farmhouse.

Aidan pulled some jeans and a hooded sweatshirt out of the wardrobe and put them on after drying himself off with a towel. The roads weren't clear enough for a vehicle, so the only way to get to the farm would have been just like how Derek did it hours before: in shifted form, straight through the woods, braving the elements. That explained why Aidan arrived rather damp and riled up.

He threw a similar outfit in Derek's direction, who also got dressed in a rush.

Despite living vastly different lives - Aidan spending all his time away from home and Derek doing a lot more physical labor on the farm, the two brothers looked very much alike. They were both extremely broad and muscular as you'd expect bears to be and had the same shade of shaggy brown hair. It was a blessing in cases like these when either one of them found themselves in need of covering up after an unplanned shift that they wore the same size clothes as well.

"Do I want to know why she was in your bed?" Aidan gave him a suspicious stare.

Always the big brother, Derek thought, *no matter how little he shows his face around here, or how old we get.*

"Get your mind out of the gutter. She's a guest. Her car crashed in the storm, knocked her out, and I brought her back here to keep an eye on her."

"A guest, eh? That's all?"

Derek shrugged, unwilling to go into the details of the matter right this moment. Actually, he wished to cut the entire conversation short so that he could go back into the bedroom to see how Clarice was holding up after the shocking display the two brothers had just given her.

"Well, perhaps if we play dumb we can convince her she was just seeing things. That would be for the best," Aidan speculated.

Derek slowly shook his head, not really in response to his brother, but more to himself. Knowing what he knew now, that Clarice did indeed have some kind of connection with him, he couldn't see how secrecy was an option anymore.

"Anyway, why don't you tell me why you're here?" Derek asked instead.

"Can't I just visit my little brother anymore?" Aidan responded gruffly.

"The way you came bursting in unannounced suggests something else is going on," Derek said while scrutinizing his brother's face. There was something there, a hint of a frown he tried hard to disguise, but Derek could still see it. Whatever he'd been up to in the nine months since Aidan's last visit, it had taken a toll on him.

"Alright then," Aidan began. "If I'm going to tell you everything, I have one condition. Don't think for a moment I'm buying the 'she's just a guest' crap, okay? I'm not stupid. You'll let me know what's going on with the human, and I'll tell you what's going on with me."

"Fine." Derek sighed. Despite Aidan's abrasive and often bossy nature, it might be useful to get another perspective on Derek's predicament anyway.

"It's a long story," Aidan said.

They walked back down the hall, past the master bedroom where he could still sense Clarice's presence. Her heartbeat had calmed down significantly. Her breathing had slowed. Even without opening the door, Derek knew that she had fallen asleep again, which was just as well.

"What do you say we discuss it over some mulled wine?" Derek didn't wait for Aidan's agreement, but just headed further down the hall anyway until they made it into the dark lounge, and from there into the kitchen, which was invitingly lit up by an oil lamp. He opened a cupboard and pulled out a bottle of mulled wine mixture he had made earlier, pouring it into a pot to warm it up. Outside, the storm had barely had a chance to calm. The wind was still whistling through the trees and around the farmhouse, and it was still raining as well.

All the while, Aidan paced up and down the room. Whatever was going on with him, it wasn't good. Derek could tell that much.

He picked up two glasses and poured the deep red, fragrant liquid into them, handing one to Aidan. They sat down around the large round wooden table and sipped their wine in silence. Derek waited until Aidan looked a bit more revitalized. If there's one thing that made bears even less chatty than normal, it was cold weather.

"She's my mate, Aidan," Derek broke the silence at last.

His brother looked up from the half empty glass, one eyebrow raised.

"I know it's not ideal, being that she's human, but I know it in my gut, and I can't fight it." Derek averted his gaze downward while continuing to warm his fingers on the mulled wine in his hands.

"I see." Aidan cleared his throat. "What does she know?"

Derek shrugged. "Nothing. I'd been avoiding the issue completely and avoiding her. But when she crashed her car earlier today, I realized I couldn't stand it anymore. I can't let her go, Aidan."

Aidan ran his hands through his still damp hair and let out a chuckle. "Believe it or not, I know how you feel."

Derek looked up. It was his turn to stare at Aidan in surprise. "How so?"

"I've also met someone. *The one.*"

"Is that why you're here?" Derek asked.

"No. Yes. It's complicated."

"Don't tell me she's human as well?"

Aidan took one last gulp before putting the empty glass down on the table and crossing his arms. "No, it's nothing like that. Anyway, your situation requires sorting out first. She doesn't know anything you say, and yet she's just seen the two of us. That's bad. Very bad." Aidan's face took on a thoughtful, more serious expression.

"I suppose, but maybe she'll be okay with it. What do you think?" Derek hoped out loud.

"It's not about whether *she* will be fine with it. What about the Code? This goes beyond just you and your *girlfriend*. The survival of our species relies on complete secrecy, as you well know!"

Of course, Aidan was right, but the tone in which he said it grated at Derek. The last thing he needed right now was a lecture from his big brother.

"Not even you can turn back time on what's already happened." Derek's face darkened as he spoke. Clarice couldn't just un-see them in their bear form, neither could he ignore the immense pull she had on him. It seemed irrational and crazy, but he knew that if he couldn't have her, he wouldn't survive his loss.

His entire situation was so unprecedented that the only comparison he could draw was with bear couples where one partner passes. The other half of the couple often died of a broken heart shortly after. Mated bears literally grew old together, or they didn't grow old at all.

"Pour us another glass. I have something to say," Aidan started.

Derek paused for a moment, tempted to argue, but finally decided to just do as he was told. Moments later, fresh refill in hand, he sat down opposite Aidan again and waited.

"I've never told you what it is I do." Aidan leaned forward and ran his fingertip across the rim of the glass, wiping a droplet of mulled wine off it.

"You've never been home long enough to discuss it. Not that I mind, you know I'm not the social type," Derek remarked.

"Obviously I've been traveling, but I never mentioned my reasons. When Mum and Dad had their accident, I couldn't shake the feeling that something else was going on..."

Derek raised his eyebrow. "You think it wasn't an accident?"

Aidan forced a smile. "You've always been sharp. Yes, that's exactly what I suspected. Of course, I had no proof."

"And you do now?" Derek asked.

"Not yet. That's why I'm here, to look through their things and the old newspaper clippings I'd kept from way back when. But what I'm getting at is, some people approached me a while ago. That's how I met Heidi recently as well."

The way Aidan said her name, Derek knew that Heidi was the woman he'd hinted at before. Aidan's mate. "Right. What people?"

"Have you ever heard of the Sons of Domnall?" Aidan asked.

"Yeah, from the old stories," Derek said.

"It would seem that they don't just exist in stories."

Derek stopped mid-sip and put his glass back down, his gaze now completely fixed on his brother.

"They're a real threat. A group of humans who know our secret and are intent on rooting us out. We're trying to form a counterpart to that. I'm now working with like-minded shifters to protect our secret and keep our own safe against the Sons of Domnall. Our group is called the Alliance."

"And how do Mum and Dad fit into all that? You think their deaths are related to what you've discovered?" Derek ran his hand through his hair, trying to make sense of it all.

"It would explain a lot, wouldn't it? The problem with us bears is, we don't organize ourselves. We tend to keep to ourselves, and when something happens, there's nobody to help out or put two-and-two together. Those who lives in packs, wolves, for example, are miles ahead of us. There have been disappearances across the shifter world. And the evidence links it all back to human interference."

Derek was stunned. Living alone in this remote part of the world, it had become very easy to assume life was quaint everywhere else. The possibility that their parents' death hadn't been an accident like he'd believed all his life was a lot to take in. And to think that their way of life was in danger because of a secret society of human assassins... That was all crazy talk, wasn't it?

"Their activities have escalated over the past few years - or perhaps it's only after the recent truce with the wolves that we've started to share the necessary information across species to find out the full extent of what's been happening. That's why secrecy is so important, now more than ever before. That's why your human poses a huge problem." Aidan pinched the bridge of his nose while looking away at nothing in particular.

"Before you burst in, and I was talking to her, I felt it. Our connection is mutual. I assumed it wouldn't be, because she's human, but..."

"We've got to know for sure. A bear would rather die than to put his mate in harm's way, but who knows how it works for humans? I'm not sure we can trust her."

"I'm sure." Derek looked up from his glass, staring his brother right in the eye. He was sure, because hidden in the dark of the doorway another pair of eyes was staring at Aidan. Clarice had woken up.

CHAPTER TEN

When Clarice finally awoke, she was surprised to still find herself in that same bed, in that same room, with the same wooden furniture from her crazy dream earlier. The only difference was the dark corner where Derek had sat was empty now, and the candle on the dresser had burnt up even further.

The welt on her forehead hurt equally, her limbs were stiff as before, and the only thing she could hear was a low howl outside the window. The storm was still going on though its intensity had reduced quite a bit.

Enough was enough. If she stayed in bed, who knows what other crazy hallucinations her mind would come up with. Clarice fought against the residual lethargy in her muscles and rolled over onto her side, ready to get out from underneath the warm covers. Her legs seemed to work just fine, even if the rough wooden floor underneath her feet felt funny, tingly, as if her feet had fallen asleep along with the rest of her.

She got up carefully, swaying slightly as she tried to maintain her balance. Then, putting one foot ahead of the other, she slowly walked around the bed and straight towards the door. *Where was the bathroom?*

Clarice turned the handle, then stopped to listen for any sign of another presence inside the house, before heading across the hall to the first other door she could find. She heard nothing but the wind. The house itself was completely quiet.

As luck would have it, the first door Clarice tried was indeed the bathroom. The mirror allowed her a first look at the damage done to her head. It looked pretty bad. Shades of blue and purple colored her skin with a bright red cut in the center. She would have expected more blood, meaning that someone - Derek probably - had cleaned her wound after carrying her here.

That was what had happened, right? Or had that also been a dream?

Clarice washed her hands, shivering as the icy cold water prickled against her skin. She hoped that the cold water would wake her up, to help her filter through her memories to determine what was real and what had just been fantasy.

"I'm losing it," she said to her reflection, then shook her head and dried her hands on the fluffy towel hanging beside the sink.

Still confused, she left the bathroom again and was greeted by muffled voices coming from the far end of the corridor. Now that she felt a bit more limber, she tiptoed her way down the hall. She'd had no idea where in the house she was before, but as she neared the room at the end, she could see shadowy outlines of two armchairs and a sofa. Further ahead was a doorway with light filtering out of it. The kitchen.

Two broad-shouldered figures sat across the heavy wooden table she'd observed through the window during her evening walks around the garden outside. One was Derek, the other one she didn't know, but the similar build and hair color, as well as the familiar tone in which they spoke to each other suggested they were related. His brother perhaps?

She overheard them talk of secrets and of humans finding out. It was surreal, but it dawned on Clarice that just maybe, her memories from the bedroom earlier weren't just part of a crazy dream after all. She couldn't quite explain how she picked up on it, but a certain sadness hung around Derek, who sat with his back towards her. The other guy, Aidan, mentioned their parents' death, and it all started to make sense.

Although it was wrong to eavesdrop, she couldn't tear herself away from the conversation. As the two men spoke, she didn't just listen with her ears, but with her heart as well if that made sense. That added dimension was so different from anything she'd ever felt before; it made the act of spying irresistible. She stepped ahead and felt her perceptions of Derek's state of mind intensify.

"... A bear would rather die than to put his mate in harm's way, but who knows how it works for humans? I'm not sure we can trust her," Aidan said.

"I'm sure." Derek radiated confidence as he spoke. Their minds were somehow connected at that very moment. He knew she stood behind him, and she knew that he knew.

Although she initially hadn't been sure whether she wanted her presence to be discovered, now her concerns were wiped away. Derek turned and smiled at her. Her heart warmed at the realization that she at least had a little bit of insight into his feelings now, even if she couldn't explain why.

"You're awake."

"Yes." Clarice stepped ahead into the light radiating from the oil lamp in the center of the table.

Across the room, Aidan looked up at her, and she finally could have a proper look at him. A strong jawline, like Derek, messy brown hair and eyes that betrayed the capacity for great cunning as well as kindness. He was handsome in his own right but had nothing on Derek of course. He looked skeptical but didn't say a word.

"I couldn't help but overhear some of that," Clarice

started.

Aidan raised an eyebrow and folded his arms.

"I don't know what happened between us, or how any of this works exactly," she addressed Derek now. "But I do know it's not just a phase, or something that'll easily pass. I feel you inside me, trying to connect with me. I can't ignore it."

Clarice glanced back up at Aidan again. "Your secret is safe. I couldn't tell anyone if I wanted to. Plus, do you think anyone would believe me?"

Although Aidan's expression suggested that he wasn't yet convinced, that didn't matter to Clarice at all. It was Derek she was concerned with, and the look he gave her now was halfway between pride and primal lust. When their eyes locked, she could clearly feel his intentions. *You're mine,* she thought. Or was that his thought rather than hers? Either way, she didn't know how she was going to deal with all this stuff coming from him, without acting on her most basic instincts.

He stared at her, as she stared at him. So much to see, so many hidden depths in those brown eyes that had sought to avoid her earlier.

Aidan cleared his throat as he got up from his chair. "I think I'm going to give you two some space."

Neither Derek nor Clarice so much as answered him. In their newfound connection to one-another, any third parties, family or otherwise, clearly held very little importance anymore.

"You can sense me," Derek said.

Clarice didn't need to nod her answer, but she did anyway out of habit.

"I've been able to feel you for days," he added.

This revelation put a smile on her face. A smile, which as it turned out, Derek could scarcely resist.

He got up, the heavy chair falling backward onto the stone floor with a loud crash. Neither of them flinched or looked back as he charged ahead, cupping her face with his large, surprisingly gentle hands and leaning down for their first kiss.

From the first touch of their lips, Clarice felt unlike anything she'd ever known. Fireworks, butterflies, electric jolts, all those terms could not begin to describe the sensations coursing through her veins. It was as if Derek's being infiltrated hers, irreversibly leaving his mark on her.

They couldn't hold back any longer, hungry kisses led to a feverish exploration of skin. His hard, muscular torso enveloped her in an embrace that made her feel tiny for the first time in her life. Tiny, yet safe, and dangerously out of control.

He ran his hands over her curves, taking his time, while his tongue teased hers, pushing her anticipation of what was yet to come higher and higher. He tasted sweet, with a hint of spice, and completely irresistible. The slight tickle on her face from his beard didn't distract. Instead, it heightened her pleasure.

As they continued to explore each other's bodies, slowly peeling layer after layer of clothes off and admiring their discoveries, Clarice knew that there would be no going back after this. She wouldn't be able to turn her back on how he made her feel.

The little glimpses into his life and past she'd gotten from the overheard conversation gave her some sense of the man. The rational part of her brain knew that there was so much more yet to find out. Would she like what she found? Her heart screamed yes while her mind was aware of the risks, but it seemed not to matter. Whether she liked it or not, fate had already set her on this path with no choice in the matter.

Having already removed his hooded sweatshirt and finding that he wasn't wearing anything underneath, she couldn't believe her luck. All the fantasies that had crept up on her during those dark hours just before it was time to get up in the morning were coming true. His body was a work of art. Hard, chiseled lines and fluid curves of muscle that could put a Greek god to shame.

Derek McMillan was the kind of man who could have easily been cast as a Gladiator in Spartacus, a show Clarice had watched less for its artistic merit and more for the eye candy. The only difference was that he wasn't as smooth and artificially well-oiled as the actors in the show, which Clarice thought was a good thing.

Here in front of her stood not a photoshopped fantasy of a man, but a real one. Hers.

As he started to remove one of the last barriers between them, Clarice's t-shirt and jeans, it occurred to her that this was usually the point in new relationships that she'd dread the most. Although she didn't like to dwell on her insecurities, she couldn't always suppress the worry that a new partner might not like her as much naked as they seemed to with her clothes on. She always feared to see a little flinch or frown, or worse, complete indifference as Alan had shown towards the end.

Derek was unlike any other partner Clarice had been with, though. He didn't just continue on the path they'd set for themselves, kissing, tasting, and worshiping every inch of her exposed skin. He did so with an enthusiasm she couldn't even have foreseen in her wildest dreams.

When she looked at his expression, as he circled her nipple with his tongue, she couldn't see a hint of hesitation or disappointment in him. Everything was right between the two of them, just as it should be. They were both equally in awe of the perfection they'd found in each other.

He stopped what he was doing when he noticed her staring at him, then cupped her face again for further kisses. The urgency with which he pressed his lips against hers made her heart ache for him. Never before had she felt so wanted, so needed, so...

"I've never felt this way before," she whispered.

He didn't answer, not using words anyway. Instead he scooped her up into his arms, sweeping her off her feet figuratively as well as literally. Only two words entered her mind, their connection growing even clearer than before. *Me neither.*

She felt weightless and unusually small again as he carried her through the dark lounge and down the hall, back into the bedroom she'd woken up in just minutes earlier. He laid her down on the soft covers, crawling on top of her on all fours. She was ready, as was he, to consummate their union in every possible way.

CHAPTER ELEVEN

Derek gazed down at Clarice's face. She looked beautiful, almost angelic if he ignored the bruise on her forehead. Her hair was fanned out over the pillow, and her eyes glistened in the soft candle light. The rest of her was equally perfect.

He'd never thought much about it before, what his dream woman would look like, but he knew already that Clarice was all he'd ever want. Her endless curves invited exploration of a more tactile kind, whether using fingertips or even his lips, and he could no longer resist her. Both bear and man wanted just one thing, to claim her and make her his.

It was impossible not to think of her in terms of his mate, the one fate had picked out for him, but even otherwise she was an attractive woman. The fact that she didn't act like she knew made her even more irresistible. Derek appreciated beauty like the next guy - bear or human- but had never had much patience for vanity.

The sweet scent of her arousal, the one he'd got but a hint of earlier, filled the room completely now. She was ready, aching for him as much as he ached for her. He noted how much her pupils had dilated, and how her cheeks had flushed to a deeper shade of pink.

She parted her legs, not brazenly, but almost involuntarily as if she was acting on instinct alone. It was a sight to behold. Her entire body seemed to invite him in while her eyes begged for further affections. Meanwhile, she was on her own journey of discovery, tracing her fingers across his biceps, and his firm, muscular chest, exploring the inked patterns on his shoulder.

He ran his hand over the ivory skin of her cleavage, taking care to be gentle with her. She wasn't the first female he'd been intimate with - even if it had been a while - but she was his first human and seemed all the more fragile for it.

As much as he tried, one part of his anatomy refused to entertain the notion of a gentle coupling. His cock had swelled to a size that was impressive for a bear, never mind a human. He hoped beyond hope that he wouldn't hurt her when the time came.

They'd reached that moment, which hung right in between endless possibility and painful anticipation. His hand traveled downward, circling her belly button, then moving on further until it reached the soft, inviting curls of her mound. So silky. Like a cub's fur. He slipped his finger in between her folds, thrilled to find that she was already wet for him.

"Stop teasing me," she pleaded, as she struggled to keep her urgent breaths under control.

Her fingers twitched, fingernails scraping skin for just a moment, before she ran her palm across and down his chest, over the ridges of his washboard abs. It was then that she finally touched his cock for the first time.

He was rock solid, had been for a while already, but the tension in his manhood was threatening to grow out of control now. As her fingers closed around his thick shaft, his mind was wiped clean of any remaining thoughts and speculations. Nothing mattered anymore except her pleasure.

Derek closed his eyes and took a deep breath in an attempt to swallow the desire to break free from her touch and plunge into her already. No, there could only be one first time, and he was going to do things properly.

He pulled away from her and crawled downward on all fours. Although her lips continued to tempt him, he wanted to taste a different part of her now. He kissed, nibbled and licked his way down, edging ever closer to those curls he had touched earlier. Every touch of his lips was met with a moan of hers.

She was vocal, yet another thing about her that he was pleased to discover.

He gently parted her legs wide enough to allow him to position himself between her thighs. Then he dove in for his first taste. Her sex was slick with sweet nectar, which he lapped up hungrily. She writhed against the sheets as he licked her outer lips first, then circled inward further and further until he finally slipped his tongue inside of her.

She tasted of honey, made of the sweetest summer flowers. The perfume of her arousal surrounded him and seduced him in a way that nothing - and no one - had ever done before. He didn't pleasure her orally as a favor to her, but because his deepest, most powerful desires demanded that he do so.

Clarice grabbed hold of the sheets, tugging at them violently as he continued his exploration of her most intimate depths. A fever-like feeling descended over Derek, clouding his mind with a red haze that made it impossible for him to think clearly. His inner bear was in charge, and somehow he knew exactly how to push Clarice's buttons.

As he alternated between licking her deeper and teasing her clit with the tip of his tongue, she reacted more and more intensely until finally she had reached the edge of her control. With her back arched, and hips raised up against his face, her moans had turned to cries, and her ragged breaths paused just for a moment.

"Oh my God!" she cried out while reaching for his hair,

tugging at it just hard enough to be pleasurable in a primal, almost painful manner.

He pulled away to get a better look at her expression but knew better than to stop his affections completely. With two fingers inside of her, and his thumb resting against the base of her clit, he drove her all the way over the cliff and into sweet relief.

With that, they'd unwittingly completed half of the journey all fated mates must undergo to finalize their bond: a selfless gift, the pleasuring of one partner by the other without expecting the same in return.

But as soon as she'd caught her breath, Clarice no longer seemed satisfied lying on her back. Derek observed her as she leaned up on her elbows and let her eyes focus on him again. She licked her lips - a gesture that he knew would keep driving him crazy as long as he was alive - and beckoned him to crawl up on top of her again.

"That was amazing," she breathed against his lips, before leaning further up for another taste of him. "Let's see what else is in store for us tonight."

Derek shuddered as her hand closed around his cock again and directed it straight at her slick entrance, his head coating itself in her sweet nectar. She bucked her hips, causing his thick cock to press against her harder though he couldn't quite enter her yet. He worried about hurting her, but the look in her eyes told him he had no choice but to proceed. She would accept no less than all he had to give.

He lowered himself, waiting as her body adjusted to him. The sensation as he finally entered her hot pussy was indescribable. It was as if he hadn't just entered her body, but invaded her mind as well. Her pleasure became his pleasure. They fed off one another, snowballing until it combined into one, and neither could tell anymore where one individual ended, and the other began.

Much to Derek's surprise, as well as Clarice's, judging from the expression on her face, her body accommodated his entire length and girth with ease. *As though we're made for one another*, Derek thought. *We are*, Clarice responded.

He started to move, each thrust of his met by a twitch of her hips. Even with her legs spread wide, he felt the stranglehold her pussy had on him as if trying to keep him inside of her as long as possible.

Derek loved how she felt against him; she provided the softness that his hard muscle lacked. Yin and yang, feminine and masculine, so different and yet so perfect together. With every move of his, he couldn't keep his eyes off the effect it had on her curves. He loved how her full breasts quivered when he pushed into her, as though they were teasing him, begging for attention.

He dove down and took her nipple into his mouth, eliciting a more primal groan from her lips. She was helpless again, pinned to the bed by his large physique, her thighs spread as wide as they would go, feet attempting to lock around his waist but having difficulty hanging on.

She reached out for his shoulders, running her fingernails over his tattoo. Her touch gave him shivers. Every move, every affection was as if it had been carefully choreographed. One paused, and the other took over, their bodies laboring away towards that common goal: complete surrender.

It started deep inside him; a twitch, which grew into a whirlwind of intense sensation that soon filled his whole body, before spilling over into hers. Sticky like honey, their pleasure clung to everything as it progressed, filling their veins, until their entire beings had been set alight.

A deep, primal groan left his lips, met by a cry from hers. Their movements sped up for a couple of strokes until Clarice's nails dug deeply into Derek's back. He shuddered into her, his cock twitching as he buried his seed into her depths.

When they opened their eyes again, they found themselves sitting upright: Clarice was held up firmly in Derek's strong arms. Their connection was complete. Selfless pleasure followed by the exchange of fluids and synchronized release.

They were spent, yet he refused to let her go, continuing to cradle her in his embrace until at last, their bodies relaxed, and they decided to lie down. Derek on his back, Clarice pressed up against him with her arm across his chest.

Clarice rested her head on Derek's shoulder and sighed deeply. Derek could hear her heartbeat slow down until it almost reached its normal rhythm.

"You must have a ton of questions," Derek remarked, as even Clarice's breaths had calmed back down.

"I imagine perhaps so do you."

"You write?" he asked.

Clarice smiled and nodded. "And you bake cakes."

"Who doesn't like cake?" Derek retorted with a grin.

"Nobody, I imagine." Clarice frowned as she collected her thoughts, and then raised her head to look up at him. "How come you're in my head? Is it always like this?"

"As far as I've heard, yes. I had no idea it would work with humans as well..."

"Mhmm... It's weird. Nice, but still a bit weird." Clarice chuckled.

"You must know, I never planned for this. I never expected to find someone I'd want to settle down with." Although Derek knew she felt the same, it was still awkward saying that kind of thing out loud.

Clarice let out a short laugh. "To think I came here to

get away from people..."

"What's waiting for you back home?" Derek asked.

Clarice paused for a moment, her thoughts racing, though Derek couldn't pick up on any particular one of them. "Actually... Nothing much. My work is flexible, and I'd been planning to look for a different flat upon my return. The one where I'm living now already didn't feel quite right anymore."

Derek wanted to ask about the phone call that first evening, his worry that there was someone else in her life but bit his tongue. There was no need to pry further. She was here with him, and that was all that mattered. In time, they'd learn everything there was to know about each other.

He wrapped his arm around her tighter, enjoying the feeling of her soft, almost silky skin pressing against his side. She was his mate now, and nobody could get between them, especially once they'd make things official.

"I have to ask..." he started.

She raised her head slightly, looking him in the eye. "It's funny, knowing what you're going to say most of the time. Yes, I'd love to stay."

As he kept gazing into her amber eyes, Derek thought he could see a change in her. There was a new brilliance in her gaze, a sparkle. It wasn't subtle like you hear about but obvious to him like it would be to any other bear. No longer did she look completely human, but her eyes seemed to glow in the dark. Like the embers of a fire that had stopped burning brightly, but refused to extinguish itself completely.

"How does it work?" she asked. "You can change at will?"

"It takes a bit of practice to control the bear side of things, but yes."

"There are so many stories about werewolves, but I'd never heard of a werebear before," she remarked.

"We like to keep to ourselves away from people. Wolves are much more common."

"So there are actual werewolves too?" Clarice sighed and rubbed her eyes with the back of her hand. Obviously she was still feeling the effects of her earlier ordeal, as well as the sweet exertion he'd just put her through.

"Yes, though I doubt you'll ever meet one. We don't exactly get along, bears and wolves."

Before she had a chance to ask another question, she was interrupted by a low rumble originating in her stomach. "I'm so sorry," she mumbled, an embarrassed smile forming on her lips.

"I'm the one who should be sorry. I hope you like stew?" Although Derek didn't want to let her go, he jumped into action anyway and got up from the bed. How could he be so selfish, forgetting about her basic needs in his eagerness to get her into bed?

She sat up as well, observing him as he hurriedly put on the bare minimum of clothes.

"Stew sounds great."

Derek waited as she put on her panties, as well as a t-shirt of his that was so big it came down almost to her knees. Then they both headed for the kitchen, hand in hand, certain that no matter how many questions still needed to be answered, everything would work itself out.

EPILOGUE

Although Clarice had had the chance to get used to the idea of werebears for a few days now, the prospect of meeting Derek's only relatives, other than Aidan, was still weird and unnerving. They were bears as well, of course, and what little interaction she'd had with Aidan before he left suggested that not all bears would be too pleased that one of their own was pairing up with a human.

They had good reason to be suspicious if you took into account the stories they'd grown up on and the fact that they had few unique rules or laws of their own except the code of secrecy. At the same time, Clarice couldn't see how the powerful bond she shared with Derek could ever be considered bad.

Derek had quickly become her entire world.

Of course, she still had her writing; after a couple of days of rest following the accident she had been able to finish her novel and get it to her editor on time to meet the deadline.

She also still had Lily, her best friend, who found the idea of Clarice's whirlwind holiday romance quite bizarre. Clarice felt some regret that she couldn't confide in Lily, but she'd sworn to keep Derek's true nature a secret and so she wouldn't be able to break that trust no matter what.

Still, Clarice also felt bad that Lily couldn't be there on the day that her connection with Derek would be made official.

Bears didn't care much for tradition, and as such there were very few rituals and ceremonies they performed regularly. One of them, the most important, was the mating ritual.

Derek had explained it to her as basically a wedding for bears and their mates. Because they lived in such isolated places and didn't interact with many fellow bears, mating rituals were small affairs, often only involving the couple themselves and perhaps the occasional relative.

Today would be no different. Derek and Clarice would perform the ritual, under the watchful eye of Derek's elder cousin, Elise and her mate, Jack. Aidan - although invited - couldn't make it, which was just as well because Clarice was nervous enough already.

She looked in the mirror one last time, scrutinizing the long chiffon dress she'd purchased for the occasion. Her brown wavy hair she'd kept down, adorned only by a few flowers Derek had picked for her earlier. He really was quite the romantic when he wanted to be. Her make-up was also kept to a minimum, just how Derek liked it, but Clarice had insisted on disguising the remnants of the bruise on her forehead with some foundation anyway.

You're beautiful just as you are, he'd said when she'd fretted over what to wear for today. Although it sounded like a cliché, he managed to say it in such a way that had completely convinced her.

Despite everything, it was still a bit surreal knowing that a man as gorgeous and built as Derek would admire her so completely. If she didn't feel it in her bones every time he was near, she would have had a hard time believing it. Things like this didn't happen to women like her, normally. Then again, normally, you'd never believe that shapeshifters existed either.

It's time, Derek's voice entered her thoughts. He was waiting for her in the hall. She could sense him clearly, even if she couldn't see him yet.

Elise and Jack would be waiting outside in the garden.

Derek had told her earlier that this was where the ritual was going to take place. The two of them would walk out together when the time came.

She smoothed down her dress, took a deep breath and opened the door. There he was.

Derek's eyes locked onto hers, and she felt herself fill with confidence. It was weird, different, how Derek could still her worries and insecurities just with his presence. She'd never felt that with any of her boyfriends from before, especially not with Alan. The more she thought about her past, the more convinced she became that everything up to this point had never felt quite real enough as if it had all just been pretend and make-believe.

I love you, she thought. He responded with a smile and offered her his arm.

Together they walked along the broad hallway, through the lobby and out the main entrance of the farm, where an impressively tall middle-aged couple waited for them, just as Derek had foretold.

The woman turned, revealing features very similar to Derek and Aidan - the eyes, the shape of her nose, all were familiar. It was obvious that they were related.

She smiled and nodded at Clarice. The man, Jack presumably, just waited in place without looking back at the two of them. A stone giant, Clarice noted with a smile.

Clarice and Derek walked across the tree-lined lawn together, taking their position across from the couple and turned to face each other. It was chilly outside, as one would expect the weather to be in early October in the Scottish Highlands, but the excitement of their upcoming union had caused Clarice's skin to burn up so much that the cold failed to affect her.

Elise stepped ahead and handed each of them a pouch. Derek had explained what to do with the contents already, so Clarice knew to open hers, taking out the first of the two items inside.

"Derek," Clarice whispered, her voice shaking with residual nerves. "Please accept this, a red rose, as token of my love, and along with it my promise to walk beside you as your mate and mother to your cubs, as long as we both shall live."

Derek's eyes remained fixed on hers, the intensity in his gaze filling her stomach with butterflies.

"I do," Derek answered, his voice slightly hoarse with emotion. "Clarice, please accept this token-" Derek pulled out a short, very aged looking dagger from his pouch and presented it to Clarice with both hands. "This blade, to keep with you for protection at all time, as a symbol that I'll always look after you as your mate and father to our family, as long as we both shall live."

As often as Derek had gone through the exact words with Clarice, their meaning had not lost gravity. If anything, she felt his intentions more deeply now than before.

"I do," Clarice responded. She wedged the dagger carefully in between her belt and the soft fabric of her dress, just as Derek had taught her to do earlier. Once back inside she would keep the weapon safe somewhere, available to her whenever she would need it - which hopefully would be never.

Now, it was time for the second item, something that was a lot more familiar to most humans, including Clarice. The rings. Clarice pulled the bigger one out of her pouch, weighing it in her hand. It was made of white gold and was very heavy; the peculiar spiral design ensured it would expand and become big enough to fit Derek's finger even after shifting.

Derek followed suit, holding up the much more

delicate counterpart meant for Clarice's finger. Hers was a simpler, non-expanding design, adorned by a cut ruby set on top.

"With this ring, I become yours, and you become mine." Derek slipped the precious ring around Clarice's finger, the sight of it sparkling against her pale skin almost taking her breath away. Although the design didn't look all that unusual to Clarice's eyes, Derek had explained that any bear would recognize it as a mate's ring, a clear sign that she belonged, even if not everyone would approve.

"With this ring, I become yours, and you become mine," Clarice repeated, putting the bigger, more masculine and complicated ring onto Derek's finger, while trying but failing to conceal the tremble in her hands.

Next to them, Elise's emotions took over, and a sob escaped her lips. "Remember when we did this, Jack?" she whispered. From the corner of her eye, Clarice could see Jack taking her hand into both of his. The stone giant evidently had a soft spot after all.

A few years down the line, who knew, perhaps Clarice and Derek would be the more experienced couple, remembering their own special day while observing another bear perform the ritual with his mate, Aidan perhaps?

Clarice looked up at Derek, whose face failed to hide the pride and admiration he felt for her. They were one now, officially. A lone tear collected in the corner of her eye as she realized the importance of what had just happened.

Human marriages ended in divorce more often than not, despite most people going into them with the best of intentions. With Derek, there was no doubt in her mind that they were truly destined to be together. Their connection would never fade because something held them together that ran deeper than the shallow infatuations people tend to mistake for love. Fate. Or biology, whatever you choose to believe in.

They would be mates forever, and nobody would ever come in between them. She tiptoed, and they shared a kiss, not because it was tradition, but because they couldn't help it.

Then, Elise came up to the two of them and congratulated them, hugging Clarice tightly and welcoming her to the family. Jack shook her hand, as well as Derek's but remained mostly quiet, nodding his congratulations at the two of them. *That went well,* Clarice thought, relieved not to have to deal with any disapproval from Derek's relatives.

As all four of them made their way back inside the house, the phone rang. *That'll be Aidan.* He'd declined their invitation, stating he had urgent business to attend to but said he'd give his best wishes on the day. She kept her senses locked on Derek as he walked into the kitchen and answered the phone, focusing as best she could to try and figure out if her assumption was correct.

"Hello?" Derek said.

Yes, that's Aidan all right, Clarice sensed, as she entered the room behind Derek.

Almost instantly, Derek's mood, which had been triumphant and celebratory until now, turned darker. She couldn't tell what was going on, but his emotions tugged and pulled at her, telling her that something had gone horribly wrong.

"I understand. I'll be there." Derek hung up and looked over at her.

Problems? Clarice thought. Derek crossed the distance between them, resting his hands on her shoulders upon reaching her.

"Aidan needs my help. His mate is in trouble. I'll ask Elise and Jack to stick around while I'm gone. I'm so sorry about this."

She nodded, sad to see him leave without the chance to celebrate their new status, but there was no room for jealousy or speculation in her mind. She could feel that the situation was serious, and the thought to question Derek's actions didn't even occur to her. There was no room for secrets between them, so in time, she'd hear all about today's troubles as well.

"Go. I'll be fine. Just..." She tiptoed to reach him again, wrapping her arms around his shoulders tightly. "Be careful," she whispered.

Derek returned her embrace, kissing her forehead a couple of times before releasing her again. "Of course. Everything will be fine." He forced a smile, but Clarice didn't feel it. There was a change about Derek, he was tenser than she'd ever seen him before, almost hostile, though of course not towards her.

He was readying for a fight, and there was nothing she could do to help.

I love you, please come back to me, Clarice thought.

Always, Derek responded.

With that, he made his way to the lounge to talk to Elise, leaving Clarice in the kitchen.

Everything was going to be fine. It had to be, right?

***

ABOUT THE AUTHOR

Dear Reader,

Thanks for reading Scottish Werebear: An Unexpected Affair, Book 1 in the Scottish Werebears Series. Although this was my debut paranormal romance release, I'm not new to writing in general. In fact, my mom still tells me to this day about how I would make up stories, and attempt to record them in my clumsy, shaky handwriting from the moment I learned to read and write. From there I went on to write fan fiction and other stuff meant for my own eyes only.

I've always enjoyed stories of the paranormal. Vampires, shape shifters, witches and magic, all featured in the books I loved the most, even when I was still growing up. But it wasn't until much later that I got into romance. One of the first writers (a self-published author just like me!) I came across was Tina Folsom, via her Scanguards Vampire series. I was hooked. From there I went on to read more paranormal romance until I found a new favorite kind of hero: bear shifters, like the kind written by Milly Taiden, Zoe Chant, and T.S. Joyce. What I love about bears is how they can be all strong and independent, a bit reclusive, and almost grumpy, but they always end up having a heart of gold (plus they tend to know their food, and we all know that a man who can cook is doubly sexy). All that (except for the shifting into a powerful bear) almost exactly describes the sort of man I ended up falling for and marrying in real life, so it's no surprise that this is what I started my publishing career with.

To find out more, check:

LoreleiMoone.com (And why not sign up for the newsletter to be the first to find out about new releases.)

You can also get in touch with me via Facebook (search for Lorelei Moone), or email at info@loreleimoone.com.

I also write contemporary romance as L. Moone. If that's something you're interested in, you can take a look at LMoone.com.

x Lorelei

www.ingramcontent.com/pod-product-compliance
Lightning Source LLC
Chambersburg PA
CBHW070451170726
48291CB00005B/1703